Despite her irritation with him, Willy couldn't help admiring his muscular build; couldn't seem to take her eyes off of his large, capable hands as he jacked up the SUV, loosened the lug nuts, and replaced the tire. Fifteen minutes later, he returned to her, looking sexy and angry, rain dripping from his hair.

"You're all set."

"I'm sorry to be such a nuisance. Here." She opened her purse and pulled out a twenty-dollar bill. "Let me pay you for your time."

"Put your money away, Sis. I don't want it."

"Oh, please. I insist."

"You might better put that toward a new set of tires," he growled. "Especially if you're going to be out gallivanting on roads like this." He turned away from her and started the truck. "Have a safe trip home."

Seeing she'd been dismissed, Willy climbed out of the truck. The man waited for her to fire up the Explorere, and then drove away without a backward glance. Willy stared after him until he disappeared from view.

"Mister," she murmured, "You are a whole lot of unusual." Driving away, she realized she hadn't even gotten his name.

What They're Saying About Waiting For The Rain........

"There aren't enough words for me to use when describing how much I loved this book. The writing is brilliant, the characters are so real and what they experience is at times heartbreaking, and at other times, joyous. The ending will have you believing in miracles." --- *Recommended Read Plus from Romance Reader At Heart*

"Darby and Willy come alive in this tale of passion, love and the supernatural. Ms Pike's tale will capture your heart!" -- *ParaNormal Romance Reviews*

"I dare any lover of strong heroines not to fall in love with Willow Mackenzie and her assortment of strange and colorful friends. The paranormal edge to this tale is gentle and subtle. The twists and turns will leave the reader involved from beginning to end, they unfold delicately throughout the story."-- *The Long And Short Of It Reviews*

Champagne Books Presents

Waiting For The Rain

By

M. Jean Pike

This is a work of fiction. The characters, incidents and dialogues in this book are of the author's imagination and are not to be construed as real. Any resemblance to actual events or persons, living or dead, is completely coincidental.

No part of this book may be reproduced or transmitted in any form or by any means, electronic or mechanical, including photocopying, recording, or by any information storage and retrieval system, without permission in writing from the publisher.

Champagne Books
www.champagnebooks.com
Copyright © 2007 by M. Jean Pike
ISBN 978-1-897445-21-1
August 2007
Cover Art © Chris Butts
Produced in Canada

Champagne Books
#35069-4604 37 ST SW
Calgary, AB T3E 7C7
Canada

Dedication

Everything, always, for Todd.

Acknowledgement

I would like to express my sincere appreciation to those who walked beside me on my journey to bring this project to completion. Marge McCoy, who taught me how to write my name at age four, and who, for the next forty years, made me believe I was capable of greatness. Noah Bowdy and Todd Pike, whose wood splitting, squirrel hunting, and wrench turning provided me with a model for male behavior. Donna Thompson and Loretta Proctor, who suffered through my early drafts. Your input was invaluable. Brenda Hill, a phenomenal writer and a wonderful friend. Thanks for not letting me quit.

One

Willow Mackenzie was looking for an eagle.

She crept along the winding dirt road, her hopeful gaze sweeping across the horizon. It wasn't like her to be impulsive, but eagles' strength and quiet majesty had always captivated her. Magical and magnificent, the eagle was the only animal brave enough to stare into the face of the sun, or so the legend said. Willow had always wanted to see one in flight. Since her visit with Dr. Chan the month before, the desire had magnified in importance. But then, everything she'd ever wanted to do had magnified.

She shot a glance into the dense, pine forest on her left, another into the open meadow on right, then up at the darkening sky. The newspaper article said the bald eagle had been spotted in a quarry outside of Murphy's Crossing, less than fifty miles from the city, but she had the sinking feeling she'd made a wrong turn and was lost.

A dull headache nagged at the base of her skull, and she pressed down on the accelerator, deciding to call it a day. Less than a mile later, she heard a loud pop and her SUV jerked to the right. Feeling the thump, she eased off the gas and coasted to the side of the road. A flat tire. *Damn!*

"And here you are, Willy," she murmured, "miles from civilization. Perfect." She flipped open her cell-phone and punched in her best friend's number. Since it would be more than an hour's drive from the east side of the city, she was going to owe Sid big time for this. When the call didn't ring through, Willy realized with a sinking feeling that she was too far out of range to obtain a signal.

She threw the phone back in her purse and sat for a long moment, rethinking her situation. There was no point in backtracking. A mile behind her, the road dead-ended in a gully. She scanned the length of the rutted dirt road that stretched out ahead. Not a house in sight. With a sigh, she climbed out of the SUV, opened the tailgate, and retrieved the tire iron and the jack from their compartment. She spread the objects out on the floor and stared at them. *OK, now what?*

She had never, in her twenty-eight years, learned to change a flat tire. For the first twenty-three, she hadn't owned a car, and for the last five, she had counted on Tom to deal with such inconveniences. Tom, who was supposed to love her in good times and in bad. The good times were fine, but he ran, like the coward he was, when things got tough.

Sadness welled up inside her, followed by anger, and she firmly pushed them away. There was no point in falling apart. Self-pity certainly wasn't going to help her out of this jam. And sitting on the side of a dead-end road wasn't going to get her anywhere either. She would just have to walk. With no other options, she grabbed her purse and umbrella, a garish, pink thing Sid had bought in New York City the summer before, locked the SUV, and set off down the road.

After the first mile, Willy's feet began to ache. An earlier thought came back to mock her, the thought that had set her on this ill fated journey in the first place: *From now on, every day will be an adventure.* She chuckled. *Some adventure,* she thought, removing her sandals. A wave of dizziness engulfed her, and the road blurred before her eyes. *Oh, Lord, please... don't let me faint.* Taking it nice and slow, she pulled herself upright, taking deep breaths. She scanned the adjacent field in search of a place to sit and rest. A rotted tree stump peeked out from the weeds, and Willy crept toward it. *You can do this, Willy,* she told herself. *Just put one foot in front of the other. That's the way.*

Halfway across the field she heard a tremendous crashing in the brush and froze. *A bear?* The sound grew louder as the animal, or whatever it was, approached. Willy felt her knees buckle. *Get a grip, girl!* As she peered in the direction of the noise, a creature bounded from the woods, a creature with a monstrously large head and a big, furry body. Using the only weapon available, Willy flapped her umbrella at it.

"Get out of here!"

The creature stopped in mid-stride and stared at her, and the breath Willy had been holding whooshed from her chest. It was a dog. A very old dog, at that. Willy's threatening stance, coupled with her harsh tone of voice, caused the animal to cringe. He cowered before her, tail between his legs. He'd merely been coming to say hello, and now Willy felt like a bully. "I'm sorry. Did I scare you?"

The dog answered with a hesitant flip of his tail. He was a chocolate lab, his muzzle almost completely gray. A patch of white ringed his neck beneath a ratty red collar, as though years of chafing had rubbed the fur away. *An old, worn out dog,* Willy thought. *Certainly not any kind of threat.* As the dog regarded her with his cloudy eyes, a thought came to Willy and she smiled. If there was a dog, then an owner had to fit somewhere into the equation. Someone who fed and cared for the animal. Hopefully someone with a phone.

She dropped to a squat and stretched out her hand. The dog approached cautiously, sniffing the air. "Where do you live, boy? Can you show me?"

He licked her hand, as if to say that all was forgiven. Willy's sense of vertigo returned, and she eased herself down to the ground. The dog sat at her side, quietly licking his feet and waiting. After a few moments the dizziness passed, and Willy stood. "Okay, come on, boy," she said, lightly slapping her thigh. "Let's go home."

Willy talked to the dog as he trotted along beside her on the road. She felt easier now, less alone. "You certainly do live in the boondocks, don't you? Nice for a dog, but it can't be very convenient for your owner. I mean, if she should run out of bread or coffee." Willy paused for a moment to survey the quiet beauty around her. "It's pretty, though. Peaceful. I've always lived in the city. My whole life."

They came upon the rotting carcass of a woodchuck, and the dog stopped to investigate. Willy wrinkled her nose as the stench of decay assaulted her. "Oh... that's disgusting."

As if in agreement, the dog moved on, and Willy resumed her conversation. She knew her constant stream of chatter was foolish, but the morning's events had unnerved her, and talking made her feel less anxious.

"You're probably wondering what I'm doing way out here."

The dog moseyed to a tree, lifted his leg, squirted, and returned to Willy's side.

"The truth is I was hoping to see an eagle. I read in the paper that one had been spotted somewhere out here. I don't think it was this road, though. I must have taken a wrong turn somewhere. I'm really very bad at--"

The dog made an abrupt beeline to the side of the road and disappeared into a thick tangle of brush.

"Where are you going?" Willy called, hurrying after him. "Hey, wait! Don't leave." She scrambled through the brush in pursuit of the dog, brambles grabbing at her long hair, while branches slapped her face and hands. She stopped for a moment to finger the angry welt rising on her cheek but continued on, fear of losing sight of the dog propelling her through the scrub. Keeping her eyes on his retreating figure, she didn't notice the tree root jutting from the ground until it caught her heel and sent her sprawling. She crawled the last few feet until the brush thinned and she found herself in a meadow. Rising slowly to her feet, Willy surveyed her surroundings with wonder. Across the field, a small cottage sat nestled in a grove of trees. The sight of it nearly took her breath away.

"Oh... how lovely," she murmured. Even the famed English cottages she'd seen in Devon could not compare to the beauty that lay before her. She'd never seen anything quite as striking, and she silently cursed herself for having left her camera in the truck.

It wasn't the cottage itself that captivated her. The dwelling was small and ordinary, and what she could see of it was unpainted. What caused her to stare was the veil of profusely blooming, blood-red roses that had overtaken the entire front of the house. It was strange and serene, as if nature had wrapped the cottage in a loving embrace. The foliage that concealed the front door was so thick and lush that Willy wondered how it would even be possible for anyone to get inside. Studying the house, she realized with an inexplicable thrill that no one lived there.

From the looks of it, no one had for quite some time.

The windows were dusty and bare of curtains, and the small wooden broom that rested beside the door was tangled in vines. Her gaze wandered to the sign that was propped in the tall grass against the propane tank. Bold black letters shouted: *For Rent.* Walking over to it, she pushed away a handful of weeds and made a mental note of the name listed on the sign. Hanrahan Realty.

This is it, an inner voice whispered. *This is the home I have searched for. The home I have waited a lifetime to find.* The thought came with an intensity that surprised her. She certainly hadn't come up Baker's Gully Road looking for a cottage to rent.

A crack of thunder tore through the quiet, pulling her from her thoughts. The dog barked. Gazing across the yard, she saw him waiting just beyond the house, at the end of a rutted dirt path, his tail beating furiously. Feeling the first drops of rain splash her face, she opened her umbrella and hurried toward him.

The path led through a grove of pine trees, then to a covered bridge that spanned a wide, chortling river. Just beyond the bridge, Willy could see another cabin, this one made of logs. Most of the dwelling was concealed by trees, but the thin curl of smoke escaping the chimney told Willy the cabin was inhabited. The dog stopped in mid-stride and pricked up its ears, then took off on a dead run toward the cabin. Willy followed at a slower pace, wondering where the old dog got his energy.

~ * ~

Fine looking were the first two words that came to mind.

Unusual was the third.

Darby Sullivan stood on his front porch and watched as the woman approached. Her pink umbrella flapped in the wind, and her long, strawberry blonde hair danced across her shoulders as she walked. She made a lovely, if comical, picture and he couldn't help wondering what her business was. As far off the beaten track as he lived, he didn't get many visitors. And definitely none as attractive as this one.

Lucky bounded ahead of the woman. He reached the porch moments later, barking joyfully and shaking the rain from his coat. With his tail whirling, he looked over his shoulder at the approaching woman, then back at Darby, as though expecting praise. As though he'd brought his master a wonderful gift... a succulent rabbit, or a plump pheasant.

"I'd like to thank you for the shower, sir," Darby said, affectionately scratching the old lab's head. "And just so we're straight, animals and birds, fine. People... not so fine." With a last swish of his tail, the dog settled himself at Darby's feet to wait.

By the time she reached the porch, the girl was out of breath, and her pretty face, drained of color. In an instant, Darby's gaze skimmed her five feet, seven inches of height, processing the way her blue jeans hugged her nicely rounded hips and the pleasant fullness of her breasts before returning to her amazingly green eyes. He noticed the way her hand shot out to grasp the railing, as though she were dizzy. He watched all this, and waited.

"Hello," she finally said.

He nodded.

"My name's Willow Mackenzie. Willy, for short. I'm sorry to trouble you, but I've had a flat tire a few miles back. I was wondering if it would be all right to use your phone." Her gaze looked beyond him into the open door of the cabin and he firmly pulled it closed.

"What sort of car do you drive?"

"It's an Explorer." Her long, slender fingers moved through her hair, coaxing it back into place. "I have a spare. I just don't know how to use it. If you'll let me use your phone to call a friend, I'll get right out of your hair."

He liked her hair, liked the wild, sun-drenched look of it, and the way it curled in damp little ringlets around her face. He liked the flecks of gold in her eyes, which at the moment were staring at him, waiting for an answer.

"Wait here," he said. "I'll bring the truck around."

"Oh, you don't have to--"

Ignoring her, he stepped from the porch and walked around the back of the house to the barn, where he kept his truck. He certainly didn't need a woman hanging around, asking questions, though he had to admit she looked as though a spot of rest would do her a world of good. He didn't like the pallor of her skin. *Young, healthy woman like her,* he thought, *hiking a few miles shouldn't do her in like that.* But of course, that was no concern of his. *Just do your good deed for the day, Sullivan,* he told himself, *and then send her on her way.*

She was waiting on the porch, and stood when he pulled up in front of the house. Letting the truck idle, he got out and opened the passenger side door for her. "'Bout five miles back, did you say?"

"Not more than that." She started to climb in, lost her balance, and stumbled. His arms shot out, encircling her waist.

"You all right, Sis?"

"I'm fine." She gave him an unconvincing smile. He held her for a moment more, liking the way she felt in his arms, and the sweet smell of her hair, then reluctantly released her. When she was safely in the passenger's seat, he slid behind the wheel. She gave him an embarrassed grin. "Sorry about that."

"No need to apologize. Are you sure you're all right?"

"I'm fine." She said it forcefully, and he couldn't help wondering whether it was to convince herself, or him. He put the truck in gear and steered it down the driveway, not at all persuaded she was telling the truth.

~ * ~

It took Willy a few moments to regain her equanimity. She searched beside her for a seat belt. Not finding one, she gripped the armrest. As the truck lumbered down the overgrown path, she shot a sideways glance at the driver, taking in the strong line of his beard-stubbled chin, his serious gray eyes, and the mop of longish, chestnut-colored hair, tied back in a careless pony tail. He had a sexy, wind-chapped look about him that she found appealing. He was quite possibly the best looking man she had ever met.

And old fashioned, too.

She thought of the way he opened the door for her. When was the last time anyone did that? And the way he had caught her up in his arms, breaking her fall. A delicious shiver rippled through her body.

Uncomfortable with her current train of thought, she studied the dials on the dashboard. The truck was old. Something out of the 1940s, she guessed, though she didn't know a lot about such things. Hoping to break the awkward silence, she asked him about it.

"What sort of truck is this?"

"It's a '48 Willys."

"It certainly is in great shape for its age. Do you ever show it? I mean, at antique car shows, and such?"

A hint of a frown pulled at the corners of his mouth. "No."

Seeing the conversation was headed nowhere fast, Willy turned and looked out the window. The truck crawled past the rose-covered cottage, and she caught a glimpse of the back yard. It was woodsy, sheltered by lofty evergreens and stately white birch trees. The tall grass that grew along the riverbank was speckled with wildflowers of blue and gold. Not content to stay in their beds along the riverbank, recalcitrant plots of tiger lilies sprawled into the yard, claiming it for their own. The sight filled Willy with a longing she could not fathom, and she cursed herself again for having left her camera behind.

"Do you know anything about this place?" she asked.

"No."

"I noticed it earlier. The truth is, I've been looking to move out of the city, and I've kind of fallen in love with this little cottage. It seems so peaceful. So--"

"It's abandoned. No one has lived there for a long, long time."

"I noticed a For Rent sign in the yard, beside the propane tank. I just wondered--"

Without warning, he slammed on the brakes. She faced him in surprise, and saw anger flashing from his eyes.

"You shouldn't have been snooping around up there!"

Willy felt her own anger flare. "I wasn't snooping. I was only--"

"Trespassing. That sort of thing might fly in the city, Sister, but not out here."

Willy stared at him, utterly flabbergasted. A hot retort burned on her lips, but she remembered she was at his mercy. If she angered him further, he might just dump her out and be on his way; then where would she be? She struggled for a moment with her temper, then said, more calmly, "I didn't mean to trespass. Your dog ran into the yard, and I followed him. That's when I noticed the sign."

The explanation seemed to satisfy him. He let off the brakes and the truck resumed its slow journey down the path. She assumed the subject was closed, and was surprised when he brought it up again.

"The real estate company has probably given up on it by now. A few people have moved in. None have stayed. Not for long, anyway."

"Because it's so far out?"

"Because it's haunted."

"What?" She gaped at him, trying not to smile. "Are you serious?"

He shrugged. "That's what they say."

She turned and peered out the back window for one last glimpse, but the heavy brush concealed the cottage from her view. She glanced at the man again. She would have liked to ask him a few more questions about the cottage, but his stony demeanor told her the discussion was over.

After a short drive, they came upon her Explorer. By that time it was raining profusely. The windshield wipers beat furiously at the steady stream of water, trying to clear a path across the glass. As the old truck pulled in behind hers, Willy opened the door. She pulled her key ring out of her purse and pressed the unlock button. The Explorer responded with two spastic beeps. "Stay put," he said, getting out of the truck.

Willy watched as he retrieved the spare and the jack and went to work. Within minutes, he was soaked through. Despite her earlier irritation with him, Willy couldn't help admiring his muscular build; couldn't seem to take her eyes off of his large, capable hands, as he jacked up the SUV, loosened the lug nuts, and replaced the tire. Fifteen minutes later, he returned to her, looking sexy and angry, rain dripping from his hair.

"You're all set."

"I'm sorry to be such a nuisance. Here," she said, opening her purse. "Let me pay you for your time." She pulled out a twenty-dollar bill.

"Put your money away, Sis. I don't want it."

"Oh, please. I insist."

"You might better put that toward a new set of tires," he growled. "Especially if you're going to be out gallivanting on roads like this." He turned away from her and started the truck. "Have a safe trip home."

Seeing she'd been dismissed, Willy climbed out of the truck. The man waited for her to fire up the Explorer, then drove away without a backward glance. Willy stared after him until he disappeared from view. "Mister," she murmured, "you are a whole lot of unusual." Driving away, she realized she hadn't even gotten his name.

Two

By the time Willy reached the city limits her head was pounding. She pulled into her hotel parking lot and went straight to her room, not bothering to stop at the front desk to collect her messages. Once inside, she opened her prescription bottle and swallowed three of the large, orange pills, knowing they wouldn't touch the pain, stripped down to her underwear and crawled into bed, her arm draped across her throbbing forehead. Rain drummed against her windowpane, adding to her somber mood. She lay completely still, willing her knotted muscles to relax.

Unable to find the sleep her body craved, she allowed her thoughts to drift back to the rose-covered cottage. She conjured up images of long, lazy evenings spent sitting on the screened-in porch, sipping lemonade and listening to the shushing of the river, while the day slowly slipped away. The thought was a pleasant one, and it made her smile.

Of course, the arrangement would have its drawbacks. *Aside from the minor little detail that it's haunted,* she thought with a smirk. The house was twenty minutes from the nearest town, if you could even call Murphy's Crossing a town.

After the debacle on Baker's Gully Road, she'd

driven back into the village and stopped at a service station to top off her gas tank and get a much needed cup of strong, black coffee. From what she'd seen, Main Street consisted of a post office, a used book store, a diner, and a large, whitewashed church. On either side of the thoroughfare, clusters of small, untidy houses squatted on their crumbling foundations. The social center of the village seemed to be its dilapidated fire department. No theaters, no concert halls. The town didn't even have a grocery store, for heaven's sakes.

Her thoughts wandered to the angry, sexy man who'd served as her unwilling hero. As handsome as he was, her new neighbor would likely irritate the hell out of her. It would make much more sense to just stay in the city.

And finish out your days in a generic hotel room, a troublesome inner voice whispered. *With a television for company, and a parking lot for a front yard?*

Stop thinking like that, Willy! she admonished herself. *Dr. Chan said the key to recovery is a positive attitude, remember?*

She sighed. Tom had offered her the condo, but the truth was she didn't want it, couldn't bear the thought of living alone in the place where she and Tom had been so happy for the last five years. At least, she thought they'd been happy...

She allowed her thoughts to linger for a moment on her failed marriage. Her anger flared again. She would not take responsibility for Tom's infidelities. Not this time.

In the end, they put the condo on the market, and within two weeks, sold it to the first couple who looked at it. Splitting the profits with Tom hadn't exactly left her a fortune, but the money from her share of the sale would probably be enough to rent the little cottage for six months. Which in her case might add up to a lifetime.

Willy, stop it!

Realizing her current train of thought was doing little to improve her mood, she focused again on the cottage. Lovely images of sunny afternoons and cool, quiet evenings calmed her and eased her aching head. She knew she was being foolish, but unable to reign in the beautiful fantasies that had taken root in her mind, she got out of bed and picked up the phone. She glanced at the clock on her night table. Four-thirty on a Monday. Most businesses should still be open. Even in Murphy's Crossing.

She dialed directory assistance and asked for the number for Hanrahan Realty. She punched it in, praying as she listened to the dull ringing on the other end.

Please... Let something work out for me. Just this once...

Her prayer was interrupted by a sharp, female voice. "Hanrahan's. Doris speaking. How may I help?"

"Hello, my name is Willow Mackenzie. I'm calling about a cottage you have for rent on Baker's Gully Road."

"That would be Abe's listing. Hang on, I'll see if he's still here."

Moments later a male voice came on the line.

"Yeah. Abe Larson here. How can I help?"

Doris obviously hadn't filled him in. Feeling mildly irritated, Willy repeated her request.

"Oh, that would be the Sullivan place. No, that's not for rent."

"I was there this afternoon," she said, tethering her irritation. "I saw the *For Rent* sign with my own eyes."

He sighed. "I'm gonna level with you, ma'am, the place is a nightmare."

She rolled her eyes. "I know, I know. It's haunted."

"Well now," he said, a hint of amusement coloring his voice, "I wouldn't know anything about that."

Willy gritted her teeth, feeling foolish for having mentioned it. "Well, what *would* you know about the property, Abe?"

"It's owned by an ornery old cuss by the name of Sullivan. It's worse than pulling teeth to get him to rent it out. Don't know why he listed it in the first place. The last few people that have inquired, he's turned away on a flimsy excuse. Myself, I think he's losing his mind."

"I'd be willing to pay six months rent in advance, if the price is right. I can assure you, Mr. Larson, I won't cause the old man any trouble."

"He's real tough to get in contact with. Lives way out in no man's land, doesn't even own a phone."

Not my problem, Willy thought.

"And with the price of gas these days, well... it's a long ways out there just to be turned away."

Again, not my problem.

Seeing she wasn't going to let him off the hook, Abe Larson sighed again. "All right. I'll try to get hold of him, but don't get your hopes up."

He took her telephone number and hung up with the agreement that he would call her with an answer by the end of the week. As she replaced the phone in its cradle, Willy felt her fiery, Irish determination spark, and she smiled. She would have the little cottage.

One way or another.

~ * ~

Darby raised his axe above a length of hickory wood and brought it down with a thunderous crash. The sun shone, hot and glaring, overhead, and he paused for a moment to wipe the sweat from his eyes before retrieving another block of wood from the pile. His axe crashed through it, splitting it easily. He'd just built up a nice, steady rhythm when he heard a car clatter down the path. Hearing the racket, Lucky lifted his head. He pricked up his ears and glanced at Darby, his old eyes filled with questions.

"It's all right," Darby reassured him.

He set down his axe, took a swallow of water from his canteen, and went to investigate. He was only mildly surprised when he saw the burgundy colored sedan sitting in front of his cabin. He'd expected the visit. Just not this soon.

A hefty, red-faced man got out of the car and approached him, mopping his face with a hankie. He extended a meaty hand. "Mr. Sullivan. I don't know if you'll remember me. I'm Abe Larson, with Hanrahan Realty."

Darby folded his arms across his chest. "I remember you."

"Is the old man around?"

"Nope."

The man fought to hide his annoyance, and failed badly. "When will he be around?"

"Tough to say. He lives in a VA home up near Buffalo. Only comes home every once in awhile. I think I told you that the last time."

"Yeah, I guess you did, at that."

Darby held Abe Larson's gaze and waited for him to state his business.

"Okay, here's the deal," he said, all traces of his earlier politeness gone. "I've got another potential renter for him. Called me on the phone two days ago, and she's real interested. She seems like a nice young gal, and she's willing to pay six months' rent upfront. You tell the old man this is the last time I'm going to come traipsing out here. If he doesn't rent to this one, the next time I come out, it will be to collect my sign."

"Fair enough."

"He can get in touch with me at this number," he said, handing Darby a business card. "I'll need his decision by Friday."

As Abe Larson huffed back to his car and drove away, Darby flicked the business card into the weeds. "The answer is no, Mr. Larson. Same as last time."

He returned to his woodpile. As he resumed chopping, he thought of Willow Mackenzie's pale, pretty face. He lined up another block of wood and sent his axe crashing through it. If only she hadn't gone poking around and seen the sign. He could have told her the owner was on an extended vacation. Damn it, he'd thought telling her the house was haunted would scare her off. Obviously it had only made the cottage more desirable. He reached for another block, remembering the way she stumbled while getting into the truck. The girl wasn't well. He'd sensed that right away, felt the subtle threat of illness in her slender body.

"I can't be expected to take the whole world on my shoulders," he growled.

Lucky's eyes flicked in his direction, then looked away.

Darby glared at him. "What?"

The dog laid his head on his paws, pointedly ignoring his master. Darby buried his axe in the tree stump and stalked back to the house. In the kitchen, he grabbed a bottle of beer from the fridge, removed the cap, and guzzled it down. Wiping the foam from his mouth with the back of his hand, he retrieved another bottle and carried it to the porch.

Renters had come and gone, over the years. Though the setting was serene and life was good here, Murphy's Crossing wasn't exactly ripe with job opportunities, and the hour's commute to the city wore most people down after a while. Most hadn't stayed more than a year, not long enough to cause him any trouble. Until Marilyn.

After Marilyn he'd put the signs away, vowed he'd never rent out the property again. He didn't need the money. The houses were paid for ten times over. The extra cash from the rental property came in handy when the town and county taxes came due, but after Marilyn, the money hadn't seemed worth the risk.

He'd turned dozens of potential tenants away. Any other time it didn't bother him. *What makes this woman so different?* He knew the answer, of course. The difference this time was that Willow Mackenzie needed this house... needed its healing, its love. She needed it as badly as he did. As he swallowed the last of his beer, his gaze wandered across the river to the cottage. Maybe it would be all right.

No, it won't be all right!

He had come to enjoy his solitude, his aloneness.

But if you kept your distance...

He thought again of Willy's eyes, her beautiful eyes.

No, it just wouldn't work out.

He wrestled with himself for the remainder of the day, and by evening, his innate compassion had won out over his fear. He would let Willow Mackenzie rent the cottage for six months. He would keep his contact with her to a minimum. She wouldn't even have to know who owned the place. Let her think there was an old man moldering away in a convalescent home somewhere, like everyone else. It would be easier that way. If he caught sight of her across the river, he wouldn't acknowledge her, wouldn't spend unnecessary time with her. Time would lead to talking, and if he talked too much, his secret would come out. And there was no way he was going to let that happen. Not again.

Three

I'm going to have my cottage. My lovely little cottage...

Willy could hardly contain her excitement. When Abe Larson called, early that morning, she thought for certain he would tell her the plan was a no-go. When he informed her that the old man had consented to a six-month rental, she nearly fainted. The prospect of spending half a year tucked away in the country seemed like a dream come true. But later, when she emptied her savings account to make the rent payments, her near-zero balance scared her senseless. What was she thinking, laying down her last penny on a property out in the middle of nowhere? Had she lost her mind?

By afternoon, her emotional pendulum had swung back to elation. The cottage was the sort of house she'd always dreamed about and the fact that her prayer had been answered seemed a good omen. It gave her the courage to face what lay ahead, to do what needed to be done, no matter how much it frightened her. With this thought firmly in mind, she drove into the parking lot of Woodland Hills Cancer Treatment Center. She sat for a moment, taking deep breaths, willing her racing pulse to return to normal, then slid from the driver's seat and walked toward the front entrance.

The modern stone and glass structure sat on a beautifully manicured half-acre of land, looking more like a golf course than a clinic. Golden sunlight shone down from a flawlessly blue sky, adding to the false illusion that Woodland was a happy place. On another day, Willy might have stopped to admire the stunning beds of geraniums and coreopsis, or to watch the family of ducks that bobbed in a nearby pond. But not today.

She stepped through the double glass doors and into a bright, cheerful reception area. The thirty-something woman who sat behind the desk fit the decor perfectly, with her compassionate eyes and pretty pink dress. Willy couldn't help thinking that under other circumstances they might have been friends. She approached the desk, hesitating to clear her throat of the lump that had formed. The woman looked up from her paperwork, and noticing Willy, gave her a warm smile.

"May I help you?"

Yes. Tell me there's been a terrible mistake. Tell me that my tests were somehow mixed up with someone else's. That I can wake up from this nightmare I've been living...

The woman's smile dimmed, as though she'd read Willy's thoughts.

"I'm scheduled to start chemotherapy treatments today." It was the first time Willy'd said the word out loud, and she nearly choked on it.

"What's your name, hon?"

Willy cleared her throat a second time. "Willow Mackenzie."

"All right, let's see..." The woman checked the appointment ledger in front of her. "Oh yes, here you are. I'll just need you to fill these out before we get started, Willow."

She handed Willy a stack of forms and directed her to a nearby waiting area, an airy, white room with plush turquoise carpets and chairs upholstered in a matching shade. Willy sighed as she sifted through the papers, most of which were duplicates of forms she'd already filled out countless times. Fifteen minutes later she returned the documents to the reception desk, where a nurse wearing a steel gray afro and a loud purple smock chatted with the receptionist.

"Willow, this is Josie," the receptionist said. "She'll be assisting with your treatments today."

Josie smiled. "We're all set, sweetie pie. You can come right on back." She marched Willy down another long corridor, humming as she went, as cheerful as if they were going to a party. When she'd taken Willy's blood pressure and her vital signs, Josie led her down another hallway and into a small, cozy room. The entire south wall was dominated by an enormous plasma screen television. On an opposite wall, a polished cherry table sat beside a deep, leather recliner. A silk floral arrangement of pretty pastel daylilies and a painting of a seascape finished off the decor. The room could easily have been mistaken for a rich woman's sitting room, if not for the medical equipment that sat discreetly in the corner.

As daunting as the experience was, the facility was a much more pleasant environment in which to receive her treatments than the city hospital, and Willy knew she would be forever indebted to Milo, her employer.

She'd gone to work at *Horizons Magazine* at age twenty-two, when the magazine was ten years old. With circulation dropping, Milo Henny, owner and senior editor, wanted a fresh perspective for his travel journal. With her uncanny eye for color, and her steely determination to succeed, Willy had quickly earned the older gentleman's confidence. He liked her style, and the youth and vibrancy her pictures brought to his magazine. Though she was young and inexperienced, he'd given her the most coveted assignments: photographing travel destinations all over the United States and Europe. After six years, Willy was earning an obscene salary and had a full benefits package. Milo considered her one of the most valued members of his team, and had recently begun to groom her to take his place as senior editor.

When the migraines and blurred vision started, keeping Willy bedridden for days at a time, Milo insisted on keeping her at full pay. And when she was finally diagnosed with a malignant brain tumor, he refused to accept her resignation.

"Take all the time you need, Willow," he said, balling up her letter and tossing it in the garbage can. "We'll call it an extended leave of absence."

"I can't do that, Milo, not in good conscience." Her eyes brimmed with tears. "The fact is I probably won't be coming back."

He came around his desk and gave her an awkward hug. "Medical conditions like yours can become very costly, Willow. We'll call it an extended leave of absence. That way you can retain your medical insurance for six months. Let's do it my way, and see how it plays out."

"Good morning, Willow." A slim woman in a white lab coat and a tidy French twist walked into the room. "I'm Doctor Leslie Frazier. I'll be overseeing your treatment today. I assume Doctor Chan already explained the procedure to you?"

"Yes."

"Very good." She made a notation on her clipboard. "As you know, you're on a six-month schedule, with periods of treatment followed by periods of rest. We'll be treating you bimonthly, on a three-hour regimen, at a fairly low level, but we'll monitor and adjust your dosing schedule as needed. Do you have any questions before we get started?"

Am I going to die? The lump reappeared in her throat, and Willy swallowed it down. "No, I guess not."

As the doctor prepared an IV, Josie retuned with a brochure, which she handed to Willy. "Most people like to watch movies or listen to music. It helps pass the time. Here's what we have available. Or there's lots of reading materials, if you'd rather do that." She indicated the tidy stacks of books and magazines on the table.

Feeling too restless for a book or a DVD, Willy scanned the list of CDs and decided on a collection of soft rock hits of the '70s. She settled into the recliner and pushed up the sleeves of her sweatshirt. Josie chatted about her cats as she inserted the IV needle into Willy's vein. It stung like a nest of hornets. *One more unpleasant thing I'll have to get used to,* she though with a sigh.

"If you start to feel uncomfortable there's a call bell right here on the table beside you. Don't be afraid to use it." Josie fitted Willy with a pair of headphones, turned down the lights, and quietly left the room. Willy closed her eyes and tried to think relaxing thoughts as the music of Barry Manilow filled her brain.

She took a deep, cleansing breath and allowed her thoughts to drift like butterflies.

Within moments, they alit on the rose-covered cottage.

...She waded out into the river, enjoying the cool sensation of the water and the smooth bed of rocks beneath her feet. The sun warmed her shoulders and a quiet breeze lifted her hair. In the trees along the riverbank, a pair of orioles sang in sweet harmony, while shimmering dragonflies zig-zagged from flower to flower, and chipmunks scampered in the grass. As she waded deeper out into the stream, the water encircled her waist, wrapping her in its chill embrace.

Embrace...

She climbed into the truck, already lightheaded from the hike. The running board was slick with rain, adding to her sense of vertigo, and she stumbled. The man was there, wrapping her in his arms, not letting her fall. She could feel the strength in his hands, and the whisper of his breath on her cheek, before he spoke. "I've got you."

She was safe. Protected. But vulnerable.

Vulnerable...

She'd been married for five years to a man she thought she loved, and yet, the first time in her life she'd felt completely safe, it was in the arms of a stranger.

Hot tears spilled from her eyes, and she brushed them away with her hand.

~ * ~

Darby trudged down the path with Lucky bounding joyfully at his heels. He wished he could share the dog's sense of adventure. Unlike Lucky, Darby was not looking forward to what lay ahead, but that jackass from the real estate agency had informed him earlier that morning that his new tenant would be moving in next week.

He stepped from the trail and slogged a path through the back yard. Shading his eyes with his hand, he surveyed the small cottage. The place was haunted, all right, but the ghosts were of his own making. They wouldn't bother Willow Mackenzie. Darby was the only one who could see them.

He plodded up the bank and around to the side of the house, pushed away a handful of vines and slid his key into the padlock. He pulled open the heavy double doors, picked up his flashlight, and made his way down the cellar stairs. He made a quick circuit with the flashlight, saw that everything was as he'd left it, then trained its beam on the electric box on the far wall. Once he'd screwed the fuses into their sockets, he turned on the overhead light. He primed the pump and opened the water valve, then grabbed a pile of screens from the corner and headed back upstairs.

He walked around to the front of the house, frowning at the overgrown foliage. The roses were becoming a nuisance. He considered cutting them down, but remembered Willy had mentioned she liked them. He removed the storm windows in the back of the house and screwed the screens into place, working mechanically, not thinking, just doing what needed to be done. When he'd secured the last screen, he opened his canteen and took a long drink. He replaced the cap and set the canteen on the ground before propelling himself up the stairs. The ghosts were waiting. It was time to go inside and face them.

He stepped through the back door and into the kitchen. The house had a closed up, musty smell, and he opened the windows to let in some fresh air. He cleared the cupboards of mice nests and plugged in the refrigerator. It groaned and slowly came to life. Steeling himself against his memories, he wandered into the living room.

Drab, he thought. *The walls could use a fresh coat of paint.*

To Marilyn's way of thinking, everything had been black and white, and her decorating style reflected her personal philosophy. She'd filled the cottage with chrome and glass, decorated with black throw rugs and snow white walls. His thoughts returned to Willy. The girl had an inner warmth, an earthy element that was almost tangible. He sensed in her an inner wellspring of joy, if only she knew how to tap into it.

For Willy, he'd paint the room the color of sunshine.

He moved to the bathroom and turned on the faucets until the water ran clear, then proceeded to check the sitting room and the spare bedroom. Finding nothing amiss, he pulled in a breath and walked into the master bedroom. The room where he and Marilyn had made love. The dull ache in his chest became a tearing wound as he struggled to hold back his memories.

Marilyn propped herself up on her elbow, causing her glorious mane of brown hair to fall across her naked shoulder. "Tell me something, Darby."

He looked away from her eyes, afraid of their beauty, and the questions they held. Questions he couldn't answer. "I love you."

She smiled. "I'm glad. But that's not what I meant."

"You said tell me something. I love you. That's something, isn't it?"

After sex, it seemed that Marilyn always wanted more of him. More intimacy, more pieces of his soul. He'd shared small things with her, like his favorite color, and songs that moved him to tears, but she wasn't satisfied with small things anymore.

"Why? Why is it so important?"

"How can I say I love you if I don't know you?"

"You know me, Marilyn."

"I want to know you more." She snuggled against him. "Love you more."

He sighed.

"Please, Darby. Tell me something about you. Just one thing."

Fear snaked around in his gut, and he converted it to anger. He threw off the sheet and got out of bed.

"Darby?"

"My parents abandoned me when I was eight years old. Happy?"

She regarded him thoughtfully. "Why did they abandon you?"

He pulled on his underwear, then his pants. "Christ, you don't let up, do you?"

"I'm not trying to be difficult, Darby, it's just... well, that was the last thing I expected you to say. I'm trying to understand why--"

"Because we were poor, Marilyn. Because the old man lost his job." He grabbed his shirt off the floor and pulled it over his head.

"Where are you going?"

"Because my mother was pregnant, and she already had three kids she couldn't feed. I was dead weight, Marilyn, so they cut me loose. That's four things. Four things you didn't know about me. Do you love me better, now?"

As he stormed from the room, Marilyn pulled on her robe and followed him. "Darby, wait. I'm sorry. Please don't leave."

He walked out the front door, slamming it behind him, the sheer love of her aching in his chest; hoping the confession would sate her unquenchable curiosity, but knowing it had only intensified it.

Darby backed out of the room and closed the door, wondering how he could still feel the pain so sharply, how so many years could have passed, and yet he remembered it all as clearly as though it was yesterday.

~ * ~

Willy's next conscious thought was of someone gently shaking her awake.

"Willow?"

Her eyes flew open and she saw Josie peering down at her.

"We're all finished, hon. How do you feel?"

Bile crept up the back of her throat, and she quickly choked it down. "Sick. I thought the side effects didn't start showing up for twenty-four hours. Does the nausea usually kick in this soon?"

"It can, honey. Everyone reacts differently. It might just be your nerves, too. We'll have you hang loose awhile, see if it passes."

As Josie started to remove the IV from her arm, Willy felt her stomach turn inside out. Her hand flew to her mouth. "Can you hurry, Josie? I really think I'm gonna be--" The bile rushed up her throat again and she vomited. "Oh, God. I'm so sorry."

Josie reached under the table for an emesis basin and thrust it into Willy's hands. She grabbed a cloth, ran it under cool water, and mopped Willy's sweating brow. "Okay, honey, deep breaths."

"Oh, Lord," Willy moaned, looking down at herself. "What a mess I've made."

"Nothing that can't be cleaned, honey. Here, let's get this on you for now." She handed Willy a cloth examination gown and helped her to the bathroom.

"Is there anyone we can call?"

~ * ~

She was still hugging the toilet, thirty minutes later, when Sid walked through the door, wearing a black leather miniskirt and matching tee-shirt. The heavy, glittery eye shadow and lip gloss told Willie she had come straight from work. She dropped to a squat and laid her hand on Willy's back.

"How are you doing, kiddo?"

Willy heaved into the toilet, and Sid held her hair back from her face. Hot tears spilled from her eyes. "I can't do this, Sid."

"Oh, sweetie, I know." Sid pulled her close and rocked her gently back and forth, and Willy clung to her.

"I'm sorry, Sid."

"You never have to apologize to me for anything, Willy. You know that." She grabbed the cloth, rewet it in the sink, and pressed it to Willy's forehead.

They waited it out, side by side, on the bathroom floor, Sid gently rubbing Willy's back. Willy felt the love that radiated from Sid's hands, and knew she was the only person on the face of the earth who really cared about her.

An hour later, Willy stood shakily to her feet.

"Okay, let's rock and roll."

"You sure?"

"I've got the pukes, Sid, there's nothing they can do about that here. I want to go home."

When Willy had changed into the sweatpants and tee-shirt Sid brought for her, they climbed into Sid's metallic pink Neon and pulled from the parking lot. Sid threw quick glances left and right, then merged into the flow of traffic.

"Why didn't you tell me it was today? I would have come down here with you."

"I don't know, Sid. You're busy."

"Screw you."

Ignoring the retort, Willy leaned her head against the headrest and closed her eyes. As they lapsed into silence, Willy knew that, like her, Sid was probably remembering her stint in a drug rehab center two years before, and how Willy held Sid's hand, cried with her through the endless nights, and cheered for her as she stumbled along the road to recovery. Sid always maintained that Willy saved her life, but Willy knew her reasons were purely selfish. She and Sid shared a closeness most sisters never achieved, and Willy couldn't imagine a life without her.

They'd grown up together in the same decrepit apartment complex on the west side of the city; Willy in unit Four B, with an alcoholic grandmother who never loved her, and Sid, in unit Four D, with a nineteen-year-old girl who loved her but didn't have the first clue how to be her mother. Neither she nor Sid had ever had a brand new outfit or a shiny toy. Their dolls came from rummage sales, and their shoes, from the needy bin at Catholic Charities. They were twin souls, dreamers, looking beyond the ugliness of Dobbler Park and finding beauty in the pigeons that roosted in the eaves and the dandelions pushing up through the cracks in the broken sidewalks. Sid captured that beauty with her sketchpad, and Willy, with her camera.

Willy received a scholarship to City College, where she earned a bachelor's degree in art and met Tom Mackenzie in the deal, while Sid apprenticed at a popular tattoo studio called The Blue Moon. Her mentor, Blue Sparks, taught Sid the intricacies of the craft, all the while luring her into his sordid world of drugs, sex, and raunchy nightclubs.

The road back had been hell, but Sid was making it, one step at a time.

Instead of turning onto Goodbar Street, where Willy's hotel was located, Sid navigated through the center of the city to her apartment on East Jefferson. She pulled into her parking slot and turned off the engine.

"Feeling any better?" she asked.

Willy nodded.

Sid helped her to the front door, where Chance Foley, her roommate, gathered Willy up in a hug. "How are you making it, babe?"

Willy forced a smile. "I'm good, Chance."

Chance's large brown eyes swept over her, filled with concern. "Do you want a cup of green tea?"

"I think I'd rather just lie down."

Willy had known Chance since high school, and he was one of her favorite people. She loved his optimistic outlook on life and his quiet sense of humor. He was one of the few people who understood her, and she had often thought they could have married, had Chance not been gay.

In her bedroom, Sid pulled the shades, tuned the radio to a classical music station, and lit a soothing, orange spice candle. She tucked the sheet around Willy and lay down beside her, gently rubbing her back. "I'm sorry, Willy." She blinked back angry tears. "I'm just sorry as hell. I wish I could take this for you."

"I'm going to be all right."

"I know. It's just... I should have been there for you

today. Damn Tom for letting you go through this alone."

"He doesn't know about the tumor, Sid, and I want it to stay that way."

"You should have told him. It might have made a difference."

"That's exactly why I didn't. I don't want him staying with me out of pity."

"I still think he should be here."

"Sid, can we please not talk?"

"Sorry, babe."

Willy closed her eyes and tried to sleep. For Sid's sake, she would continue to fake an optimism she no longer believed. She thought of the serpent coiled in her brain.

The chemotherapy would not kill it, only hold it in abeyance for awhile. And though the prognosis wasn't good, hadn't been good from the start, she thought she and Tom could conquer it together.

Tom...

She had known about the serpent for two weeks before she worked up the nerve to tell him. Their relationship had been strained, and her constant headaches hadn't helped. A computer technician with a major corporation, Tom's recent promotion took him out of town for days at a time. On his first night home in a week, Willy decorated the table with candles and a pretty bouquet she picked up at the flower shop downtown. She bought steaks and splurged on plump, red strawberries and real whipped cream, thinking maybe they could share them in bed, later. Though they had argued countless times over the amount of time Tom's job took him away from home, she vowed that this time she would be cheerful and supportive while he told her about his work, and when the time was right, she would tell him about the tumor. It turned out Tom had news of his own.

He was unusually quiet that night, picking at his

food, bringing her every stab at conversation to a screeching halt. After dinner, she laid a hand on his shoulder as she poured his coffee. "Is anything wrong, Tom?"

"Willy, sit down."

His somber tone caused her to sink woodenly into her chair.

"There's no easy way to say this, so I'm just going to say it. I've met someone."

She stared at him, numbly processing the information as he told her about Laci, the lovely computer software engineer he'd met a month before, the woman who was to replace her. She sat in stunned silence, until finally his hand covered hers.

"Willy, please say something."

"What would you like me to say, Tom?"

"Admit it, Willy, all of the stress between us, your constant migraines... you haven't been happy either."

She felt anger spark in the midst of her pain, but refused to rise to it. "Is that what you need to say to make this okay, Tom?"

"Damn it, Willy, this isn't easy for me, either. For once, just try to understand where I'm coming from."

She sat, hand pressed against her lips, holding back the torrent of words that ached for release. She couldn't understand, not this time. Not when she still loved him so.

"Oh, here we go with the silent treatment," he said acidly. "The wounded dove. You know something, sweetheart, that's half your problem. You're always expecting the worst. Even when you're happy, you're always waiting for someone to come and rain on your parade. I wanted someone I could share life with, not carry through it."

She fought back tears. "I don't want to say mean things to you, Tom, and I don't want you to say mean things to me. I just want you to go."

He sighed. "Okay, you're probably right. This is starting to get real ugly, and I don't think either one of us has the strength for a war tonight."

She sat at the table while he threw some clean clothes into a suitcase and walked out of her life. She didn't say a word about the serpent in her head. There was no longer any point, not when a rattlesnake had been sharing her bed.

Pressing her face into her pillow, she gave in to her tears.

I wanted someone to share life with, not carry through it...

"I'm sorry, Tom." She mouthed the words in the dark. "I'm sorry I couldn't love you the way you needed me to."

She had tried to love spontaneously, to loosen the chains she kept carefully locked around her heart. But fear was a way of life for girls like Willy and Sid. They'd grown up knowing the sting of rejection, of never being quite good enough. As a result, Willy had never taken a chance on anything that mattered, never known how to really love.

And now it was too late to learn.

Four

Willy surfaced from a deep and dreamless sleep to find daylight peeking around the edges of the blinds. She was conscious of the rattle-bang of pots and pans and the low murmur of conversation in the kitchen. She lay quietly for a moment, savoring the comfort of Sid's pillow-top mattress and the aromas of perking coffee and sizzling bacon. The nausea had passed in the night, and she realized she was starving. When she could no longer ignore her hunger, she pulled on Sid's bathrobe and padded out to the kitchen.

Sid sat at the table, sipping coffee and reading the newspaper. She glanced up when Willy appeared in the doorway. "Morning, sleepy-head. How do you feel?"

"Starved."

"That's got to be a good sign." She went to the cupboard, retrieved a plate, and piled it with bacon and scrambled eggs. "I hope Chance didn't wake you when he left. I don't know why he's got to slam the door like that."

"It's after ten o'clock. I should have been up a long time ago." Willy's glance moved over Sid's shorts and sloppy tee-shirt. "Why aren't you at work?"

"It's Sunday, Willy."

"It's Sunday?" She stared at her friend, incredulous.

"I lost a whole entire day?"

"I wouldn't say lost, exactly," Sid said with a grin. "Maybe just misplaced."

She frowned, then scraped the reminder of the eggs from the frying pan onto Willy's plate.

"Whoa, stop! I can't eat all that!"

"You're getting too thin, Will. You need to eat."

Willy started to protest, but there was no disputing Sid's observation. In the last few weeks her face had taken on a washed-out appearance, and her normally curvy figure teetered on the edge of gauntness. She had a weakness for beautiful clothes, but lately the contents of her closet hung loosely on her frame, making her look like an ill-fitted mannequin.

When Willy had consumed the entire plate of eggs, Sid handed her a bath towel and a clean change of clothes.

"I hate to break it to you, sweetie, but you reek."

Willy stood beneath the hot spray of the shower, trying to talk herself out of the headache that never seemed very far away. Twenty minutes later, dressed in a pair of Sid's black jeans and a Counting Crows concert tee-shirt, she returned to the living room to find Sid sitting on her balcony, smoking a cigarette. She stepped out into the sunshine, flopped down in a wicker chair, and picked up a magazine. "You really should quit smoking, you know," she told Sid.

"Listen, Sista, I don't want to hear it. This is the only vice I have left." Sid took a drag from her cigarette, her voice becoming sad and far away. "Real fair, huh? I sit here, smoking like a chimney fire, and you're the one who gets cancer."

They sat quietly for a moment, then Willy asked, "Does my hair look any thinner to you, Sid?"

Sid scrutinized Willy's luxurious mane. "No. Why?"

"I noticed a lot of hair in the trap after I took a

shower. And there was some on my pillow, too."

"You're gorgeous, Willy. You'd be gorgeous bald as a billiard ball. But we'll get you a wig, if it comes to that." She squinted, studying Willy's face. "I'm thinking platinum blonde."

Willy rolled her eyes. "Perfect."

"Willy, I wish you'd think about staying here with us."

"We've already been through this, Sid."

"I know. And I think you're being really bull-headed."

"You've only got two bedrooms."

"I can sleep on the couch. And Chance isn't here half the time anyway."

"I appreciate it, Sid, but I don't need you to babysit me."

"I'm not offering to babysit you. I just hate the thought of you living in a hotel room. I'd feel better having you here. Just in case something happened."

"Nothing's going to happen."

Sid took another pull on her cigarette. "Is it because of Zoe?"

"No, it's not because of Zoe. I like Zoe very much. I've told you that." Willy pulled in a deep breath, knowing Sid was not going to like what she had to say. "Anyway, it's a moot point, because I found a place. A nice little house. I signed a six-month lease on it."

Sid's face lit up. "Awesome. Why didn't you tell me?"

"It all came about pretty quickly. I just decided a couple of days ago."

"Is it on the east side, I hope?"

Willy took another breath. "It's in Murphy's Crossing."

"Jesus, Willy, now I know why you didn't tell me.

Because you knew I'd talk you out of it." Sid crushed out her cigarette, staring at Willy as if she'd lost her mind. "You can't move out to the middle of nowhere. What if you get sick again?"

"I'm not going to get sick again, Sid, because I'm not going for any more chemo treatments. And besides, I already sent the realtor a check."

"Well, then. I guess it's a done deal."

Sid sat in hurt silence, a silence Willy knew stemmed more from concern than anger. "I need a change of scenery, Sid, a quiet place to sort myself out. I can't do that in the city."

Sid didn't answer.

"I don't know why I need to do this. I just know I do. I was hoping you and Chance would help me move. When we separated, Tom got custody of all our friends."

Sid sighed. "I'll help you move. But I won't be happy about it."

~ * ~

True to her word, Sid showed up at Willy's mini-storage compartment at eight o'clock the following Wednesday morning. Chance owned a food catering service and had offered up his delivery truck, as well of one of his employees, for the day. Willy's heart sank when the driver's side door opened and Toots Wayfield got out. She had never cared for Toots. He was loud and obnoxious, always ready with an off-color joke, or a snide remark--usually aimed at women. But she supposed she should be grateful for another set of hands, no matter whom they belonged to.

With the four of them working, Willy's storage compartment was emptied in no time. Within an hour, the three vehicles were headed down the interstate; Willy led in her SUV, with Sid following closely in her Neon and the delivery truck rumbling along behind. When she reached Baker's Gully Road, Willy slowed to a crawl. She couldn't remember exactly how far up the road the cottage was. Baker's Gully was full of twists and turns, and she worried she might miss the driveway. *What if you have to call for an ambulance, Willy?* her inner voice fretted. *How will they ever find you? That is, if Murphy's Crossing even has an ambulance...* She shot worried glances into the dense forest all around her and wondered again if she'd made a terrible mistake.

She rounded another bend, and the cottage came into view. Someone had trimmed away the brush, making it much more visible from road. She pulled into the driveway and climbed from the Explorer. As she stared in wonder at her new home, a feeling of peace enveloped her, and her fears melted away.

Sid pulled in behind her, and moments later the truck coasted into the driveway.

"Welcome to the Land of the Lost," Toots grumbled, stepping from the truck. "Holy Moses, would you look at those weeds. How we supposed to get in the door?"

Ignoring him, Willy walked around to the back of the house. Abe Larson had overnighted her a key, and she was anxious to see the inside.

She unlocked the back door and stepped into the kitchen. It was small, and the appliances terribly outdated, but a bank of oversized windows on the far wall offered a magnificent view of the back yard. She opened the fridge, then checked the gas burners on the stove. Antiques, she thought, but they seemed to be in good working order. Noticing a bouquet of daisies sitting in a canning jar on the counter, she smiled. Obviously the old man had hired a woman to come in and tidy the place up.

She walked through an archway and into the living room. Despite the fact that the rose vines completely concealed the windows, blocking any outside light, the room had an open, airy feel about it. The soft wash of yellow on the walls had been added recently, she thought, detecting a faint odor of paint. She loved everything about the room, from its built-in bookcases to the wide plank floor. She was especially taken with the fieldstone fireplace that dominated the center wall, suggesting cozy autumn evenings by the fire.

Investigating further, she discovered a bedroom off the living room, just large enough to hold a single bed and a chest of drawers. Beside the bedroom was an inviting little alcove with a window seat and a rocking chair.

She discovered another, larger bedroom off the kitchen. The window had been left open, and she could hear the sounds of the river and the twittering of birds. The perfect alarm clock, she thought, smiling again. The cottage's only bathroom came equipped with the standard toilet, sink, and bathtub. The room was plain, but functional, and smelled faintly of pine cleaner.

With her tour completed, she returned to the kitchen, where Sid and Chance were already stacking boxes. "What do you think, Sid?" she asked.

"I think you're an awful long ways from a Starbucks."

"I think it's fabulous, Willy," Chance said. "Real peaceful."

"I think we should get the damn truck unloaded and get back to civilization," Toots said.

The four of them got busy, unloading the boxes first, then the furniture: a bed, a chest of drawers, and a pair of easy chairs. Finally the truck was empty, except for Willy's overstuffed suede sofa. Chance looked at it dubiously.

"I don't know about this one, Willy," he said. "We might play hell getting it through the back door. Any way we can go in through the front?"

Willy considered the sofa. It was comfortable as sin, but much too large for the room. "I don't want to disturb the roses, Chance. If that means leaving the sofa behind, then so be it."

Toots rose to the challenge in his usual arrogant way. "I can get it in there. You ladies just stand back and watch how it's done."

He hoisted the sofa from the van and dragged it across the yard, leaving deep ruts in his wake. He hauled it up the stairs, his arms straining beneath its weight, turned it sideways and shoved it through the door and onto the enclosed porch. He turned it sideways again and jammed it through the kitchen doorway. Willy heard the sound of ripping fabric, and cringed.

"Stop, Toots!" she shouted. "Can't you see it's not going to fit?"

"The hell it's not!" he bellowed. He thrust again, and she heard a terrific crash as the door casing splintered.

"Toots, please. Just bring it back out. It's too big for the room anyway."

"The damned thing is stuck, now," he grumped. "Might as well get it in, as out. Chance, if you're going to just stand there, staring at me, why don't you give me a hand?"

They wrestled with the sofa for another ten minutes. Finally, Toots cursed and threw his baseball cap on the floor. "I give up."

"You can't give up, Toots," Sid said. "She can't very have a sofa sticking halfway out her door. We've got to go one way or the other with it."

"I hope that's an offer, Superwoman," Toots bellowed, "Because I could use another set of hands, here, but I seriously doubt yours are gonna cut it."

As if summoned by the outburst, Willy heard the loud rumble of her neighbor's truck coming down path. "Oh, no," she groaned.

The truck slowed to a crawl and stopped at the foot of the trail.

"Now who in the hell is this?" Toots grumbled, but there was no mistaking the raw appreciation in his eyes as the man got out of the truck and strode across the yard, with Lucky trailing at his heels. His walk was purposeful, powerful, and Willy felt a curious thrill flutter through her stomach. As he drew nearer, she noticed him assessing the situation. His glance moved over the wayward sofa and splintered door casing before coming to rest on her face. He was annoyed. There was no doubt about it.

Lucky bounded to her side, and she bent to scratch his ears before meeting his owner's eyes. "We meet again," she said stiffly.

His gray eyes skimmed over Chance's channeled earlobes and glittering nose ring, and Willy could see disapproval in them.

"Problem?" he asked simply.

"Ya think?" Toots growled.

Ignoring him, the man stepped onto the porch.

"We seem to be in a predicament. It won't go one way or the other..." Willy's voice trailed away. He wasn't listening, anyway. He studied the angle at which the sofa protruded from the door, evaluating.

"One of you girls is going to have to climb through the doorway," he said.

Willy moved toward him, and Sid laid a hand on her arm. "I'll go, Willy. You shouldn't overdo it."

Once Sid had scrambled across the sofa and through the doorway, the man said, "Okay, what we want to do is rock it, real gently, back and forth."

They rocked the sofa in a seesaw motion. Willy couldn't keep from staring at his muscular arms as they strained beneath the sleeves of his tee-shirt.

"It's loosening up," Sid's voice called from the doorway.

"Easy does it," the man said. "See if you can slide it

back my way."

Within moments, the sofa slid back through the doorway, and the man ran his hand over the splintered wood. "I don't suppose anyone has any tools?"

"I got tools aplenty," Toots said with a lewd wink.

The man glared at him.

"I have a tool box in the truck," Willy said. She hurried across the yard, her cheeks aflame. Why did Toots have to be such an insufferable ass? She returned with a pink toolbox, the words *Woman's Tools* embossed on the front. The man opened the box and inspected the tools. Frowning, he pulled a pink screwdriver from its slot. He slid it beneath the splintered casing, gently easing it from the doorway. When all three casings had been removed, he instructed Sid to go back inside.

"Easy does it, now. We have to hook the arm through first. After that, the rest should follow without a problem." Tipping the sofa sideways, he jockeyed the arm through the doorway. The rest of the sofa slid in behind it.

"Thank you for coming to my rescue. Again," Willy said.

His eyes met hers, held them for a moment, then skimmed over her friends.

"You're welcome," he said, not a hint of warmth in his eyes. "Come on, Lucky. Let's go."

With his dog following, he strode back to the truck, got inside, and drove away. The three stared after him in silence, until finally, Toots whistled. "Man. That was one ugly dog. But the owner ain't half bad. Almost worth moving out here for."

"He has nothing to do with my decision to move here," Willy snapped. With the truck unloaded, she was wishing Toots would leave. But in good conscience she couldn't send him away on an empty stomach, even though he'd torn her sofa to shreds.

Forcing a cheerful tone into her voice, she asked, "Anyone want to do lunch?"

They locked up the house and headed for the local diner. Picnic tables with bright, checkered tablecloths had been set up behind the building, and their meals were served in yellow plastic boats. A pair of chattering old ladies stood by to refill their lemonade glasses. Willy thought it was rather charming, but Toots grumbled all through the meal, soundly spoiling her appetite.

With the last of the feast consumed, Chance groaned and rubbed his belly. "I'd love to stretch out under that tree and take a nap, but we really should take off. I have a retirement party to cater at seven."

"I appreciate your help, Chance," Willy said. "I can't tell you how much."

"What are friends for?" He softly kissed her cheek. "Be well, babe."

After Toots and Chance drove away in the truck, Sid and Willy headed over the hill to the next town to pick up a few groceries. Back home, Willy arranged the groceries in her new cupboards while Sid tore into the packing boxes. Within an hour the kitchen looked like home. Willy made a pot of coffee, and they carried their steaming cups to the porch.

"I don't know about you, Will, but I'm beat."

"I feel really good, Sid. I should be exhausted, after working all day, but I have more energy than I've had in weeks."

As soon as she said it, Willy realized with surprise that it was true. She sat for a moment, enjoying the absence of pain, until Sid asked abruptly, "What's the deal with your neighbor?"

"I don't know what his deal is. He seems kind of strange."

"Good strange, or bad strange?"

"It's nothing I can nail down, just a feeling."

"You'd better figure it out, sweetie. He's got it bad for you, you know."

Willy gaped at her. "I don't know any such thing. If anything, he thinks I'm a big pain in the keester."

"Not true, my friend. Dude's crazy about you. I saw the way he looked at you today."

"Yeah, I saw that, too. I especially liked the way he glowered at me when I came back with the tools."

Sid gave her a mischievous grin. "That's because Toots tried to hit on him."

Willy choked on her coffee. "Oh, Sid. He didn't!"

"Oh, yeah. He did." She took a swallow of coffee. "Can't really blame him for trying. If he were to loosen up a little, dude might be half cute." Sid snorted. "Oh, sweetie, you should see the look on your face."

"You can laugh, Sid. You get to go back to the city on Friday. I have to live next door to the guy."

When they'd finished their coffee, they went back inside to watch a movie. Willy's electricity was included in her rent, and already turned on, but since the local cable company didn't extend their service to Baker's Gully Road, she and Sid had rented three chick flicks at the supermarket. They made a jumbo bowl of popcorn, got into their pajamas, and spent the evening laughing like two adolescents at a slumber party. Finally, at midnight, Sid padded off to the guest room. Willy lay in her bed, unable to stop thinking about what Sid had said.

Dude's got it bad for me? What is Sid seeing that I'm not? She searched her memory, seeking evidence that what Sid said was true. An hour later, still unable to sleep, she made a cup of tea and carried it to the porch. She savored the sight of the moonlit back yard, the merry laughter of the river, and the insistent peeping of frogs, until a rustling sound in the dried leaves beside the porch startled her to her feet. She laughed softly when a furry head peeked in the door.

"Lucky? What are you doing here?"

The old dog wagged his tail and stepped onto the porch. Willy scratched his ears and sat back down, and the dog settled himself at her feet.

"So tell me... How mad is he?"

The dog bumped his tail against the floor.

"You can stay for a little while, Lucky, but not all night. I don't want him coming over here looking for you."

It was a lie. Willy knew it the moment it slid from her lips. As she sipped her tea, her gaze wandered across the river to her neighbor's cabin. She couldn't help the little thrill that came with wondering when she would encounter him again.

~ * ~

Darby sat on his front steps in the moonlight, drinking a bottle of beer.

He couldn't seem to keep his mind from replaying the afternoon's events and the loud, uncouth fellow who had come to help Willy move in. What the jackass needed was a punch in the mouth, and Darby would have been more than happy to give it to him. He wished he had never ventured across the river today.

It was plain and simple nosiness that drove him across the bridge. Seeing two men and two women, he'd naturally assumed they were couples, and wondered which man was partnered up with Willy. He hadn't wanted to admit, even to himself, how jealous the thought made him feel.

Up close, it became obvious to Darby that the two men were homosexuals. The loud jackass not as obviously gay as the one with the jewelry, but the evidence was there, just beneath his overbearing, obnoxious veneer.

Darby wasn't so far removed from society as to be

shocked. Homosexuality was becoming more and more prevalent in society, he supposed. He'd seen it firsthand overseas, and even in the army, though people were not as open about it then, as now.

His thoughts went back to the girl with the pale face make-up and the inky, black hair. Obviously a lesbian.

Willy's partner?

Darby didn't understand it, didn't believe in it. Didn't want it to be true. Not of Willy. Not when she was so nicely equipped to satisfy a man's needs.

It was a dangerous thought, and he firmly pushed it away.

It was none of his business how Willow Mackenzie chose to live her life, and if for some reason she wasn't attracted to him then so much the better.

He drained his beer bottle, refusing to acknowledge how much the idea disappointed him.

Five

By Friday morning the last of the boxes had been unpacked, Willy's new telephone was in service, and Sid had had her fill of the country.

Earlier in the week they'd discovered a small wooden table and a pair of benches in the attic, dragged them down to the porch, and eaten every meal there since. That morning, they chatted easily as they devoured plates of waffles piled high with whipped cream and strawberries-- Willy's specialty, and Sid's favorite meal.

"It's really beautiful here, Willy," Sid said, gazing across the yard. "I understand why you need to be here, but I'm going stir crazy."

Willy smiled. Knowing how Sid thrived on the hubbub and commotion of the city, she was grateful her friend had stayed as long as she had. "I know, Sid."

Sid shoveled a forkful of strawberries into her mouth. "I have to admit, there's something to be said for all of this good, fresh country air. My tendonitis hasn't flared up once since I've been here."

"M-hmmm."

"At least I feel better about leaving now that you

have a phone. Promise you'll call every day."

"Sid, I've known you for twenty-five years, and I've never called you every day."

"Well, at least every other day, then. And I want you to promise me you'll let me go with you to chemo next week."

Willy stared across the yard, not answering, not wanting unpleasant memories of chemotherapy to intrude on the beautiful morning.

"It's your decision, whether you go or not, and I'll support you either way," Sid said. "But promise you'll think about it. I know it made you feel like crap for a couple of days, but you're looking so much better. If one treatment can do that, Willy, then ten might heal you."

"I'll think about it," Willy said.

An hour later, with their breakfast eaten and the dishes piled in the sink, Sid got into her Neon and drove away. As the dust settled behind her, Willy let out a sigh of relief. She loved Sid dearly, but after spending three days with her, Willy was looking forward to some much needed peace and quiet. She breathed deeply of the flower-scented air. Despite the initial nausea, she had to admit that Sid was right. She did feel good, healthy and strong. Her glance wandered across the river. *Strong enough, even, to try and smooth things over with her neighbor.*

~ * ~

Back in the kitchen, she assembled the ingredients for a deep-dish apple pie, another of her specialties. When it was baking in the oven, she went to the bathroom and filled the tub with water. She told herself the capful of jasmine-scented bath oil she added was purely for herself. She wasn't the least bit interested in the angry man across the river. In the first place, she was still wrecked over Tom's betrayal. And even if she were interested, which she wasn't, this was no time to start a new relationship. She might not even be alive in six months.

The thought was sobering, and she pushed it from her mind. She didn't want to think such thoughts. Not today. Not when she was feeling so strong. On impulse, she dumped in another capful of bath oil. Her aim was to try and mend fences, and as they said, a person caught more flies with jasmine than with vinegar. Or something like that.

After a long soak in the tub, Willy dressed in a pair of white Capri's and her favorite green blouse; the same shade as her eyes, she'd often been told. She applied a coat of brown mascara to her lashes and a dab of apricot gloss to her lips before brushing out her hair. She had become obsessed with her hair since the chemo treatment, and found herself constantly checking for bald spots. Satisfied that it seemed as full as ever, she pulled it up in a knot and fastened it with a silver clip. When a last glance in the mirror satisfied her that she looked all right, she grabbed the apple pie from the windowsill, where she'd left it to cool, and set off down the path.

The day was steeped in sunshine, and the woods, alive with scuttling creatures and singing birds. She'd left the safety of her yard feeling unsettled at the thought of another encounter with her sexy new neighbor, but the peaceful setting quickly erased her fears.

Just across the covered bridge she came upon a cluster of bushes, loaded with plump, ripe long berries. Unable to resist, she plucked a berry from its branch and popped it in her mouth. The juice slid over her tongue like nectar, and she eagerly plucked another. She had never tasted berries so juicy and sweet before. They made her mouth water for berry muffins, and she made a mental note ask her neighbor if she could return, later on, with a bucket.

She was reaching for another berry when the breeze shifted, bringing with it a fetid stench--a gamy, putrid odor, unlike any she had ever experienced. She heard a low moaning sound, and froze.

"What on earth..." she whispered.

She stood very still, listening. The sound came again, causing the hair on the back of her neck to prickle. She couldn't identify it. It wasn't a growl, exactly, but it was definitely animal. She heard another moan, followed by a thrashing sound in the brush.

"Lucky?" she called softly. "Is that you?"

The noise stopped abruptly, and she took a cautious step. The sound had definitely come from nearby, but the breeze shifted again, making it hard to tell from what direction the sound had come. She shot a glance behind her. It wouldn't make sense to turn back. She was closer to her neighbor's house than her own. Quickening her pace, she forged ahead.

She rounded a bend in the road and froze again. An enormous black bear stood in the center of the path, raiding a patch of long berries. Two cubs played nearby, swatting at each other and growling. Mama bear gave Willy a long, hard stare before grunting at her cubs. When Willy screamed, the startled bear rose up on her hind legs. Whether she felt threatened or wanted Willy to, Willy couldn't guess.

What should I do? she thought frantically. Too frightened to know, she stood and stared at the bear. One of the cubs took a tentative step in her direction, his nose twitching, tasting the air.

Using the only decoy available, Willy set the pie on the ground and backed away.

The two cubs scampered over to investigate, and Mama Bear roared. Willy turned to run. A tangle of tree roots caught her foot and she fell to the ground. Mama Bear advanced, and Willy screamed.

~ * ~

It was making a low, growling noise.

That, and the fact that it shook and shimmied all

over the road told Darby his problem was a bad wheel bearing. He had just removed the wheel, and was reaching for the old bearing when he heard the unmistakable sound of a woman's scream. Lucky pricked up his ears and looked toward the woods. The sound came again. Darby wiped his greasy hands on a rag and threw it aside.

"Come on, boy. Let's see what she's gotten herself into this time."

He hurried down the path, and hadn't progressed more than a few hundred feet before he discovered the problem. Willy sat on the ground, a look of pure terror on her face, as a black bear and two cubs feasted on what appeared to be the remains of an apple pie.

"She won't hurt you, Willy," he said.

"How... how do you know?" she squeaked.

"Because I know." He clapped his hands at the bear. "Go on. Get out of here!"

Lucky barked, as if adding his two cents. The bear stared at them for a long moment, then turned and lumbered away, her cubs in tow. Seizing the opportunity, Lucky lunged at the pie plate, his tail whipping as he licked up the remains.

Darby walked to where Willy sat and pulled her to her feet. She looked cool and pretty this morning, her hair swept back, a hint of color in her cheeks. She smelled like fresh air and sunshine. He breathed deeply. And jasmine. She clung to him for a moment, visibly shaken. He felt her slender body trembling, and had an overwhelming desire to protect her. To offer her comfort. To receive comfort in return. He gazed for a moment into her sea-green eyes. She was a damned desirable woman, and everything inside of him urged him to kiss her.

As if sensing his intentions, she pulled herself from his grasp, something that looked a whole lot like anger taking the place of her fear.

"She wouldn't have hurt you," he said simply.

"You hear of it," she said, straightening her blouse. "Bears mauling humans. It happens all the time."

"Not here."

"I've never seen one before. Not up close."

"You get used to it after awhile."

"I can't quite imagine that," she said, brushing the dirt from her pants.

"Was there something you wanted?" He indicated Lucky, who was happily licking his chops. "I'm sure you didn't come out here to feed my dog an apple pie."

He tried to keep his amusement from his face, but she saw it.

"I baked the pie for you," she said crisply. "My way of thanking you for your help the other day."

"Well... Thank you."

"I'm really not as helpless as you might think," she said, a definite edge in her tone. "I'm perfectly capable of defending myself against a mugger, or navigating in horrific rush hour traffic. This is just a whole new realm of dangers for me."

She was damned cute, and he bit down on the inside of his cheek to hold back a smile. "Did you get all moved in?"

"Yes, I did."

"It looked like you were having quite a time of it." He added softly, "You and your homosexual friends."

He'd known it would make her angry, and couldn't think why he'd said it, except that a part of him still wanted to kiss her, and he felt a fierce need to know where he stood.

She stared at him, disbelief coloring her pretty green eyes. "My friends' sexual preferences are none of your business!"

He shrugged, angering her further.

"I'll invite whomever I please into my home, which

is *also* none of your business! And anyway, we were doing fine. Nobody asked for or needed your help."

"You were doing fine?" He let loose a short, incredulous bark of laughter. "Oh, you were doing a dandy job of it. Just for the record, lady, any time your friends try and jam a six-foot davenport into a three-and-a-half foot doorway, it becomes my business. Your *friends* splintered my damn door casing. Who do you suppose is going to have to fix that?"

"*Your* door casing?"

He saw her expression change, and immediately realized his mistake. *Damn.*

"Do you mean to tell me that *you're* Darby Sullivan? You're the man who owns my cottage?"

"I'm Darby Sullivan the Third," he corrected. "I look after things for my grandfather."

She glared at him. "Why didn't you say so in the first place?"

He glared back. "Maybe I didn't think it was any of your business."

She pulled in a breath, clearly trying to get herself under control. "All right, fine. I came over here to try and smooth things over with you. Now I'm wondering why I bothered. Thank you for letting me rent your cottage, Mr. Sullivan. You can take the money for the door casings out of my security deposit. I won't be bothering you again." She turned and marched away, leaving Darby to stare after her. He told himself it was for the best. He'd already made one slip-up. He couldn't afford to make another. But as he watched her disappear around the bend, he couldn't help regretting the harsh words that had passed between them.

~ * ~

Back home, Willy threw her soiled clothing into the washing machine and slipped into a pair of jeans and a tee-shirt. She was still fuming. Darby Sullivan was not merely old-fashioned, as she had first thought. He was narrow-minded and rude. Who was he to sit in judgment on her friends? And why hadn't he told her he owned the cottage? Why make her look like a fool?

Her face flamed as she thought of her encounter with the bear, how she'd once again been put in the position of looking silly and weak. She knew how ridiculous she must have looked, sprawled out on the ground, whimpering.

How pathetic am I?

Willy had always prided herself on her self-reliance. In addition to surviving childhood in Dobbler Park with her abusive grandmother, she'd taught herself two foreign languages and traveled throughout Europe unescorted. Reminding herself she was not the frail little fool Darby Sullivan made her feel like, she marched across the yard. One thing was for certain, she wouldn't bother him again. From now on she would handle whatever came her way. She lifted her face to the sun's warming rays. She would put the morning's encounter out of her mind and not let it spoil this gorgeous day.

She investigated the small shed beside the house and found it full of rakes, shovels, and the usual gardening paraphernalia. She dug out a hoe and a spade and went to work, digging up a small plot of ground in the front yard. Though the back yard was populated with wildflowers of every kind, Willy had always been partial to petunias, pink, purple, blazing yellow. Of all the flowers she knew, Willy loved petunias best. She decided she was going to have a dazzling display of them this summer, since it might very well be her last.

She worked until early afternoon, until she had dug up a four-foot by four-foot plot, then, satisfied with her handiwork, she got in her SUV and drove to town. She remembered seeing a fruit and vegetable market called The Farmer's Wife just outside the village. She hoped they would have what she was looking for.

Fifteen minutes later she steered into the parking lot of The Farmer's Wife and turned off the engine. The place was actually quite charming, Willy thought, an old, weathered barn, rusted tin signs nailed to the front advertising everything from motor oil to Coca Cola. In front of the barn were baskets filled with plump red tomatoes, tangles of green beans, and bulky watermelons. An oversized table was piled with flowers of every kind. Willy got out of the truck and hurried toward them.

While there seemed to be an abundance of impatience, geraniums, and pansies, the only petunias she saw were straggly and wilted, and she fought her disappointment.

"I'll give you a good price on those." Willy glanced up to see a woman in her mid-fifties approaching. The farmer's wife, she assumed, perfectly suited for her role in a white apron and a bright blue scarf, beneath which prickly pink curlers peeped. "The petunias go fast. Them are the leftovers."

"Do you have any others?" Willy asked.

"Nope, not petunias. I got some gorgeous nasturtiums in the greenhouse out back. Or maybe you'd rather have pansies, got lots of them left."

"I really had my heart set on petunias," Willy told her.

"Well, them are all I've got. Normally two-fifty a pack, but I'll sell you the bunch for twenty dollars."

Willy picked at a limp blossom, doubting there were enough good plants in 'the bunch' to fill even a fourth of the space she'd prepared.

"Make it ten for the lot," the woman coaxed.

Willy smiled, admiring the woman's persistence. "Sold."

The woman rang up the sale, blatantly looking Willy

over. "Most of the locals come in and grabbed up the petunias on Memorial Day. But you ain't from around here, are you?"

"No, I'm from the city, actually," Willy said, pulling a twenty-dollar bill from her purse. "I'm renting a house out on Baker's Gully Road for the summer."

"Pretty out that way. Which house?" She handed Willy her change, along with a brightly colored flyer, which Willy folded and put in her pocket.

"It's owned by a man named Darby Sullivan."

An old man sat in a lawn chair beside the counter. Willy had thought him asleep, but now he lifted his head and regarded her from behind a pair of thick bifocals.

"Haven't heard that name in a coon's age. Darby Sullivan, you say?"

"Yes, that's right. Do you know him?"

"I worked with a Darby Sullivan many years ago. He bought the place out on Baker's Gully right after the war. Bunch of us used to commute to the city every day. Worked in a flour mill out on Kessler Avenue."

"Now, Dad, don't you start in about the good old days," the woman said.

Ignoring her, the old man continued, "I put in twenty-five years at that mill. Married a sweet little gal, and had five children. That's my baby girl." He indicated the farmer's wife. "Lost track of ol' Darby. He quit the mill after about ten years. Can't even remember his face now, but Lord and butter, I remember bumping to the city in the back of his truck. A Willys, if I remember it. Mud brown."

"You remember it," Willy said. "His grandson still drives it."

The old man laughed at some faraway memory. "What I wouldn't give for another ride in that truck. If you should see old Darby, tell him James Weatherby sends his regards."

"I'll do that."

Loading her flowers into the back of the truck, Willy frowned. With any luck, she wouldn't be seeing the old man or his grandson ever again.

Back at the cottage, Willy removed the flats of petunias from the back of the Explorer and carried them to the garden. She arranged the better looking ones in front, and scattered the rest near the back. She stood back and surveyed her work with a frown. *Pretty skimpy. Maybe I can fill in with some violets.*

A bumblebee landed on her hand, and she quickly brushed it away. *That was close.* She thought again of the bear and her cubs. *Two close calls in one day.*

Just then she heard Darby Sullivan's truck coming down the path, and quickly turned her back. *Talk about close calls,* she thought. She'd actually found him attractive, even hoped they might become friends. She was glad Darby Sullivan had shown his true colors before she set herself up for more disappointment.

~ * ~

By late afternoon the Willys was back in business.

Having replaced the bad wheel bearing, changed the oil, and given the truck a much needed wash and wax, Darby decided to take it down the road, see if there were any more kinks he needed to work out of it. At least that's what he told himself.

The truth was he was still feeling bad about the morning's altercation with Willy Mackenzie. *Should I stop by,* he thought, *try and patch things up with her?*

Driving past the cottage, he noticed her planting flowers in the front yard, and eased off the gas. She turned her back on him without so much as a wave. *Obviously still angry. Probably just as well,* he thought, rumbling on.

He rarely went to town, but decided to drive to the gas station and top off his tank.

Maybe he'd pick up a newspaper, see what was new in the world.

A mile down Baker's Gully he passed a car. A black sedan, official looking. He'd seen the car before, the day he'd changed Willy's tire, seen it cruising slowly down the road, its driver scanning the scenery.

Looking for what?

The car made him uneasy, and he couldn't say exactly why. His military training had fine-tuned his instincts for danger.

He'd sensed it many times before, and been right.

He sensed it now, and hoped to God he wasn't.

Six

The sound of rain drumming on the tin roof of her cottage kept Willy asleep in her bed until ten o'clock on Saturday morning. Hearing the distant rumble of thunder, she opened her eyes and glanced sleepily at the clock. Seeing the time, she scolded herself and climbed out of bed. Rain or no, she had plans for the day and was already more than an hour late getting started.

A half hour later, the downpour had subsided to a light drizzle. After a hot shower and a cold breakfast, Willy was ready to go. She felt optimistic as she packed her camera and binoculars into her backpack. According to yesterday's newspaper there had been another sighting of the eagle near Murphy's Crossing.

Persistence is the key, she thought. Photographing the eagle was no longer a passing fancy. It was a quest. She'd sit in the gully all day if that's what it took.

Locking the door behind her, she stepped from the porch and cut a path across the yard. The grass felt thick and heavy and wet beneath her feet. She'd have to cut the lawn soon, she thought, or hire someone else to. She reached the front yard and stopped abruptly. A soft bleat escaped her lips. She stood for a long moment, staring, unable to believe what she was seeing.

Her flowerbed was alive.

Overnight, the bedraggled plants had exploded in vibrant color. The petunias waved in the morning breeze, a chorus line of painted ladies dancing in frilly, gypsy-skirts of purple and gold. She hurried across the yard and dropped to her knees beside the bed, fingering the velvety petals, not at all convinced they were real. Surely someone was playing an elaborate joke. *The farmer's wife?*

The petals left a sticky residue on her fingers. Artificial flowers certainly wouldn't do that. The petunias were real. Not merely alive, but flourishing; gone from limp and pitiful to bold and beautiful overnight.

But how?

Gazing upward at the hazy sky, she thanked a God she had begun to doubt existed. Who but God could have given her such a glorious gift? *One last gift?*

There you go, Willy, she scolded, *seeing the dark side again.*

She considered that for a moment. Was Tom right? Was she so steeped in pessimism that she couldn't enjoy the flowers for worrying about the weeds?

You're going to be different from now on, Willy, she reminded herself. *You're going to be optimistic. You're going to seize what time is left, squeeze every ounce of joy out of every precious moment.* She took out her camera and snapped a few shots of the flowers before climbing into the Explorer and heading for the gully.

~ * ~

It was the perfect morning for hunting, cool and damp, a blanket of wet earth to muffle his footsteps. Darby raised his rifle, breathed in, breathed out, and took his shot. Fifty feet away, a red squirrel fell from its branch in the maple tree. He gathered it up and put it in his sack with the others. Four, so far. One or two more and he'd have the makings for a nice pot of stew.

Tired of the hunt, Lucky wandered off to investigate a nearby rabbit hole. As Darby lined up his next shot, the dog pricked up his ears and gazed toward home.

"What is it, boy? Hear something?"

The dog let out a low growl, and Darby took his shot. Stuffing the last squirrel into his sack, he slung it over his shoulder and turned toward home.

A fist squeezed in his gut when he saw the mail jeep sitting in front of his house. He rarely received mail, and never any that was hand-delivered. He had a mailbox at the end of the road but he only checked it on rare occasions.

This won't be good, he thought.

The mail carrier, a youngish man wearing blue slacks and a blue windbreaker stood on the porch, peering into the window.

"Help you?" Darby said.

Startled, the man spun around, nearly losing his balance. "You can if you're Darby Sullivan. This is my second trip out here. I've got a letter for you."

The name *Crosby* was stitched on the man's windbreaker in big, gold letters. Darby's gaze shifted from Crosby's face to the envelope he held. A standard, white, business-sized envelope with a green and white flap glued to the front. *Certified.* The fist in his gut squeezed tighter. "I'm Sullivan."

Crosby eyed the rifle nervously, and Darby set it down.

"Great. I'll just need you to sign for the letter and I'll get right out of your way."

Darby eyed the envelope warily and forced himself to reach for it. He glanced at the return address. State Parks and Recreation Commission. Fear reached out and wrapped its icy fist around his throat.

Oblivious to his discomfort, Crosby tore the front flap from the envelope. "I'll need you to sign here," he said, pointing to a box outlined in green. "And print your name right here, below it."

Taking the pen Crosby offered, Darby scrawled his name inside both boxes.

Crosby shifted in his boots. "Looks like it's going to turn out to be a nice day."

Not likely, Darby thought. He handed Crosby his pen and watched as he climbed into his mail jeep and drove away.

He carried the letter inside, set it on the table, and grabbed a bottle of beer from the fridge. He sat down at the table and stared at the letter. *State Parks and Recreation Commission.* The lettering was bold and black. Big, square, no-nonsense print. Ominous.

He picked it up. It felt heavy in his hand. Unless he missed his guess, and he rarely did, the letter was connected to the black sedan he'd seen crawling around on Baker's Gully Road.

He finished his beer and went back outside to retrieve his bag of squirrels. He skinned and gutted them, then carried the meat inside. The letter stared at him from the table.

He rummaged in the cupboard for a fry pan and melted a stick of butter. He coated the squirrel meat in flour and breadcrumbs and dumped it in the pan with the butter. He cut up an onion and threw it in. The letter called to him but he ignored it. He diced a few potatoes and carrots and threw them in a stockpot. He added salt and pepper, two cups of water. He dumped the onion and the squirrel meat into the pot, covered it with a lid, and turned the flame up high. The letter on the table screamed his name.

He picked it up and shoved it in his pocket, then grabbed a box of matches from the cupboard. Retrieving a bag of garbage from the wastebasket in the corner, he carried them down to the burn pit in a far corner of the yard. He threw the bag of garbage into the pit, then pulled the letter from his pocket. He struck a match with his thumb and lit the corner of the envelope, then threw it onto the garbage. He stood back, watching, as the garbage caught fire--slowly, at first, then with a vengeance, as the flames licked hungrily at the unread newspaper he'd bought the day before. When the letter was nothing more than a curl of gray smoke in the humid air, he went back inside to check his stew.

~ * ~

By five o'clock Willy had shot three rolls of film. Sitting still as a statue, she'd managed to photograph a doe and a fawn that'd stopped to nibble at a leafy bush and a blue heron circling low above the river. She'd photographed a rabbit and a chipmunk and a black and yellow spider, along with dozens of unusual ferns and wildflowers.

Everything except an eagle.

With a dull throbbing starting behind her temples and her legs stiff from sitting, she hiked back to her Explorer, ready to call it a day. Her persistence hadn't paid off, as she'd hoped. *Maybe tomorrow,* she thought with a sigh.

Back at the cottage, the light on her answering machine winked at her from across the room, indicating three new messages. Sid was the only person she'd given her new phone number to, and she smiled as she pressed the play button. It was nice to know someone cared about her. Seconds later, Sid's husky voice filled the room.

"Hey, girlfriend. Just checking in... Are you there? ...Guess not. Hey, didn't you give your doctor's office your number? They called here today looking for you. I gave it to them so I hope that's all right. Call me later, okay?"

The machine beeped, then Sarah Peebles, Dr. Chan's receptionist, was in the room with her. "Hi, Willow. I had some trouble tracking you down. We weren't aware that you'd moved. Doctor Chan would like to set up an appointment to follow up with you after your initial chemo treatment. We'll be here until three o'clock today if you want to give us a call, otherwise we'll try to get hold of you on Monday. Thanks." Sarah's message ended, and there was a brief pause.

"Hi, Willy..."

Her breath caught. A dozen emotions collided inside her as Tom's deep, rich voice filled the room.

"I know you probably didn't expect to hear from me. Hell, I didn't even know you'd left town..." He paused, clearly agitated. Tom liked to be in charge, and Willy could almost feel his discomfort as he fumbled for the right words. "The thing is, Willy, I wondered if you could meet me at my lawyer's office one day next week. There are some residual issues about the 401K, some paperwork that got overlooked. I'd like to get them signed and witnessed so we can wrap this thing up. Give me a call on my cell and let me know what day's good for you." He recited his number, as if she didn't know it by heart, then Willy heard a soft click as he disconnected.

Her fingers trembled as she rewound the tape. She listened to Tom's message again, then again. *Wrap this thing up,* he said, as if the divorce were a pretty package, a birthday gift he was eager to give himself. Tears stung her eyes as a feeling of loss filled her soul. She realized the source of her sadness immediately. On some subconscious level, she'd hoped she and Tom could reconcile, somehow, work things out. She shivered uncontrollably as the hope grew cold and died inside her.

She moved woodenly through the kitchen, preparing a tuna sandwich and a bowl of soup she knew she wouldn't eat. She carried it to the porch and sat at the table, staring across the river. An hour later, she dumped the soup and sandwich into the garbage can. Retrieving a magazine from her bedroom, she carried it to the porch and resumed her place at the table. She did little more than glance at the pictures before shadows fell around her, and it grew too dark to see the pages.

The screen door creaked open and Lucky poked his head in, his tail wagging tentatively as his eyes sought permission to enter.

"Hi, Lucky," she said wearily.

The dog crossed the porch and rested his head on her knee.

"You have to stop coming over here," she told him. "Don't you know your master and I are feuding?"

The dog nuzzled her hand, and she leaned her head back and closed her eyes, absently stroking his head.

"I suppose I'm going to have to call him," she said.

The dog sighed.

"I feel the same way," Willy told him. "But what else can I do?"

Her first thought was that Sid must have given Tom her number, but she quickly dismissed the idea. Sid was too loyal, and being the computer genius he was, there was no information Tom couldn't hack into, if he wanted it badly enough. If he'd discovered her phone number, he undoubtedly knew her address, as well. He was likely to show up at her door if phoning didn't get the result he sought. That was the last thing she wanted. She'd have to call him. But not tonight.

It was a foreign concept, avoiding Tom, and one that would take some getting used to. Especially considering that Willy had spent a fourth of her life pursuing him.

Early in the relationship Tom liked to brag about how he'd pursued her, until finally, in a match of wits and charm, he won her over. Willy played along, knowing that just the opposite was true. Sure, Tom had wanted her at first glance, but Willy knew his wanting didn't extend beyond a night or two. With one look in Tom's brown eyes, she knew she wanted him forever.

She'd learned early on that what guys like Tom wanted most was that which was unobtainable. Though she wanted him passionately, she held him at bay, making him settle for late night study dates and occasional dinners out. The more aloof she acted, the more convinced Tom became that he couldn't live without her. And secretly, she returned his devotion one hundredfold.

His good looks and charm aside, she saw in Tom a kindred spirit, a drive to succeed that matched her own. Though Tom came from money, he shunned his familial assets, wanting to prove himself to his domineering father. They married one month out of college, vowing that together they would grab hold of the finer things in life.

Unlike Tom, Willy's determination stemmed from a basic instinct to survive. She'd learned to be self-reliant almost from birth. Her mother, just eighteen years old when Willy was born, dumped her baby daughter on her mother's cracked doorstep in Dobbler Park and walked away. She hitchhiked her way to Las Vegas, planning to earn her living as a dancer. On a rainy May morning in 1978, Meghan Malloy walked down I-390 and disappeared.

Looking at Meghan's pictures, at her bold, red mouth and the gleam of laughter in her hazel eyes, Willy could not fathom how her sour-faced grandmother had given birth to such a magnificent creature. Murphy's Law seemed to be Granny Eva's credo.

Trust no one. Take what you can get, any way you can get it. Fight for what you want, Willow, because there's always a wolf at the door, waiting to take it from you.

Willy understood early on why her mother left, but it was years before she understood why she never came back.

In high school, Willy worked in a dingy photo studio

at a discount store, taking pictures of children and dogs. She gave Eva the required fifty per cent of her paycheck and hid the other half in an old sneaker in the back of her closet. She went to college on government grants, working in an all-night coffee shop to pay for her books and clothes. With all of the nothing she'd been given in life, Tom Mackenzie seemed like a lavish gift from a very stingy Santa Claus.

She and Tom...

She'd honestly believed that together there was no obstacle in life they couldn't overcome. And now she was back to fighting alone, fighting a dark and deadly enemy she couldn't hope to conquer.

An owl hooted in a nearby tree, pulling her back to the moment. The hour was late, and the air, heavy with a musky, woodsy smell, as if someone nearby was enjoying a campfire.

~ * ~

It looked as though the whole wide world was on fire.

Thick smoke burned Darby's eyes as he hustled through the streets of what had been an ordinary village just a few hours before. He squinted hard, trying to stay focused on Perry Weidman's shoulders, a foot in front of him. There was an ear-shattering crash as something exploded nearby, and he lifted his arm to shield his face from flying debris.

"Why in the hell are they doing this?" From out of nowhere, Joe Barker was on his left. "Burning their own goddamned village?"

"I don't know."

It would have been more accurate to say he didn't care. All Darby wanted at that moment was to go home. As it was, the mission was completed. A half mile through the jungle, a truck waited to collect those of his battalion who had survived the attack, waited to carry them someplace else. Tomorrow or the next day there would be another mission. In any case, their work here was done.

He felt a sharp tug on his sleeve and stopped walking. An old woman with a leathery, sun-baked face held his shirt, her fist bunching the fabric in a tight knot. He tried to shake free of her, but she held fast, clinging to him, speaking frantically. He could not understand her words. Didn't want to try. He was weary of their words. Weary of their battle.

"Leave off!" he said, giving her a shove.

She held fast, shrieking, pointing to a nearby shack.

Joe Barker shouted at him. "Sully, come on!"

The company was retreating fast and he was falling behind. He tried to pry the woman's fingers from his clothing, but she would not be dissuaded.

He stared into her eyes and shivered, despite the blinding heat. Her eyes looked a thousand years old; old, tired eyes that had seen more than any eyes should. His gaze followed her wildly gesturing hand to the shack and he saw a face in the window. The face of a child.

Darby moaned in his sleep, tried to surface, and fell deeper into his nightmare...

Almost against his will, he turned his footsteps back toward the house. Joe Barker's hand was on his arm.

"Hell you doing?"

The child's eyes peered at him from the window, wide and wild and terrified.

"I'm going in there. There's a kid."

"Don't be a damn fool, Sully! They did this to themselves."

He stared into the woman's wise, terrified old eyes. "No they didn't."

He heard another shout as he headed into the conflagration. "Fall back, soldier! That's an order!"

Darby advanced instead.

Inside the doorway, Darby dropped to his belly and

crawled toward the window. The smoke burned his lungs and his eyes, and he could feel the heat melting the hair from his arms. Through the choking flames, he crawled, inch by inch, to save a child who would probably be better off dead. But he'd seen his eyes and identified with what they held: fear, sorrow and despair. He crawled toward the window, shouting words he knew the child would not understand. It was hopeless, but he couldn't make himself quit.

He'd seen too much of himself in the child's eyes. Groping blindly, he felt for the small figure huddled in the corner. He grabbed it, pushed its face into his chest, and crawled through the door just as the roof collapsed. Outside, he handed the child into the old woman's outstretched arms. She spoke more words he couldn't decipher. Bowing her head, she removed a chain from around her neck and pressed it into his hands. The chain held a small, silver medallion. The woman touched it gently, spoke more words. There was no mistaking the reverence in her voice.

Rough hands pulled at him, striking him hard in the face. He fell back to the ground and looked up to see a pair of angry eyes staring at him. The eyes of an officer.

"You'd better march, soldier, and you damn well better not look back again, unless you want to get left behind!"

Darby's eyes and his hands and his lungs were on fire. His eyes sought the old woman's one last time, but her eyes were closed. She spoke more words. A soft, steady stream, a chant.

Rumbling away to safety in the back of an army truck, the chain felt heavy in Darby's pocket and the medallion poked him in the thigh. As the truck lumbered through the jungle, he fingered the charm and wondered if it was worth the court marshal he had no doubt earned, disobeying a direct order. By nightfall, the jungle was a memory, miles and miles behind him. Unable to find the sleep his body begged for, Darby felt in his pocket for the medallion. It was hot, burning with a power and a promise he would not understand until many years had passed.

Seven

Gray, drizzly weather kept Willy inside on Sunday. With her plans for a return visit to the gully effectively thwarted, she spent the day sorting through her 'rainy day' boxes instead. She came across packets of photographs and letters Tom had written her, over the years: Valentine's Day greetings that proclaimed his undying love, leftover postcards from their honeymoon. One by one, she tore them to shreds and threw them in the fireplace. Each item she touched brought back painful memories, and at the end of the day she fell into bed, emotionally exhausted.

Monday brought more rain, but Willy barely noticed. She was busy taking inventory. Room by room, she took stock of her possessions, keeping the things she had bought for herself, piling the things Tom gave her in a corner of the kitchen to be boxed up and donated to charity. As the pile grew larger, so did her carefully compiled list of needs: sheets, towels, a new set of dishes. Having faced the reality that her marriage was over, she felt compelled to scour every trace of Tom from her life. She wanted no reminders of their years together, nothing he had touched.

By mid-afternoon, physically and emotionally spent, she prepared a cup of tea and carried it to the porch, along with her portable telephone. She'd called Dr. Chan's office earlier and scheduled an appointment for the following morning. She had also phoned Sid. She had one last phone call to make, and the thought of it made her feel ill.

Plucking up her courage, she dialed Tom's cell phone, breathing a sigh of relief when her call went directly to voice mail. "I have an appointment in the city tomorrow morning," she said crisply. "I could probably meet you at your lawyer's office at around two. Call me back if that's not convenient." She hung up the phone, praying he wouldn't.

She leaned her head back, closed her eyes, and listened to the rain drumming on the roof, a sound she normally enjoyed. Today the steady drone depressed her, but she supposed a certain amount of melancholy was to be expected, under the circumstances.

With tentative fingers, she traced the area at the base of her skull, pressing, moving upward, seeking outward evidence of the tumor. There were no bulges, no tender spots. The absence of pain was like a gift, one she fully expected to be revoked at any moment.

But maybe not...

She felt healthier since moving to Baker's Gully than ever in her life. Maybe the cancer was gone. Maybe the chemo and the fresh air had worked some sort of magic.

That could happen, she thought. *Couldn't it?*

Her thoughts returned to her upcoming appointment with Dr. Chan. She was hopeful for the first time in weeks, optimistic that the visit would bring good news.

The appointment with Tom's lawyer, on the other hand...

She considered calling her attorney, but decided against it. Zoe would advise her not to surrender the 401K, or at the very least, she would want to negotiate for something in return. Having lost his love, there was nothing more Willy wanted from Tom, and nothing left to contest. He didn't love her anymore. How did a woman argue with that? The appointment would be painful, but she would get through it. Then she would regroup, somehow, find a way to get on with her life.

~ * ~

Darby stood the slats of wood he'd mitered end to end, fitted them together in the corners, and studied them. Frowning, he returned the shortest of the slats to his workbench and shaved off another half inch. He checked it again.

Much better.

Satisfied with his work, he set all three pieces on the workbench and dug a can of white paint and a paintbrush out of a cabinet in the corner of the barn. He spread a coat of lacquer across the wood, congratulating himself on having formulated the perfect plan. He'd been wanting to patch things up with Willy since the incident with the bear, but had no idea how to go about it. The solution came to him that morning, and all at once the splintered door casing seemed a blessing in disguise.

He'd venture across the river tomorrow, he decided, gauge her mood, get a fix on whether or not she was still angry. If she was, he'd pretend his only reason for paying her a visit was to repair the door. That way he could find out where he stood without looking like a fool.

What's happening to you, Sullivan, an inner voice rebuked, *scheming like a school boy?* He wasn't used to being at odds with himself and wasn't enjoying the feeling. No woman had ever made him so insecure, but then, he'd never met a woman as captivating as Willow Mackenzie before.

He finished painting the slats, left them on the bench to dry, and headed back to the house for lunch. Across the river, he noticed a curl of smoke escaping from the chimney of Willy's cottage. The sight warmed him through. He liked to think of her sitting by the fireplace, cozy and warm. Safe.

He allowed himself a fleeting, pleasant image of Willy curled up in a rocking chair, logs crackling in the nearby grate. His reverie was quickly shattered by the memory of another fire, and he shuddered. He hadn't dreamed about the old woman in many years and wondered why he would now.

Because of the letter, an inner voice whispered.

The letter. Darby could think of a few reasons the State Parks and Recreation Commission might contact him, none of them good. He wished now that he hadn't burned it. At least he'd know what he was up against. Darby believed in facing an enemy square on. What in the hell had come over him?

Fear, the voice told him.

Yes, fear. His glance once again swept over the cottage. He thought of Willy, and felt again the troubling conviction that she wasn't well. A steely determination settled around his heart. He would not lie down. Whatever it was, for Willy's sake, he would stand and fight. If it was a war the Parks Commission was after, then Darby intended to see that they got one.

~ * ~

Willy was awake long before her alarm clock sounded on Tuesday morning.

Sliding out of bed, she prepared a pot of spaghetti sauce for later, then took a long, hot shower and dressed in the royal blue skirt and matching jacket she'd laid out the night before. She hooked a strand of pearls around her neck and pulled her hair into a sleek French braid. She looked in the mirror and saw a self-assured woman staring back at her and wished she felt the same confidence inside.

She hauled the boxes out to her Explorer, started it up, and headed down the long and winding road. When she reached the village, she swung into the alley behind the whitewashed church on Main Street, dumped the unwanted items in the drop box, then made a left-hand turn at the town's only traffic light and headed for the interstate.

Traffic was heavy, and by the time she reached the city a headache nagged at the base of her skull. Blaming it on stress, she parked in the lot beside Taylor/Bach Medical Center and walked toward the front entrance.

Inside, Sarah Peebles greeted her with a smile, telling her the doctor would see her shortly. A nurse took Willy's vital signs and propelled her to the scales. Her blood pressure was good and she'd gained back five of the fifteen pounds she'd lost.

Both good signs, Willy thought.

Moments later, Dr. Chan bustled into the exam room. He gave her a reassuring pat on the arm before seating himself on the swivel stool beside her. He was a compact, energetic man, barely five feet tall, with a warm smile and a sprinkling of gray in his jet-black hair. He might have been thirty-five, or fifty. It was hard for Willy to tell.

"How are you feeling, Willow?" he asked. His eyes held as much kindness as his voice, and Willy felt herself relax.

"I'm feeling really good, Doctor Chan."

"Are you sure?" A hint of doubt shadowed his smile. "You look as though you're in pain."

"I haven't been, up until today. I've been feeling great. Healthy. Since the chemo, I've been... I've moved out to the country, and it's been..." Realizing she was babbling, Willy took a breath, released it, and started again. "It's been very restful. I guess the drive in today unnerved me."

"Tranquility is good for the soul, Willow. There is no disputing that," he said gently. "But I must admit I'm feeling less than comfortable with your decision to move so far away from the city. With your medical condition, it's important that you are reasonably nearby the hospital."

Willy drew a breath. "Dr. Chan, I'd like another

MRI, if that's possible. I think...that is, I feel strongly that...that some sort of miracle has occurred."

He regarded her for a long moment. "How so?"

"I feel... I think I'm," she hesitated to say it out loud, knowing how foolish it was going to sound. "Cancer free again," she finally blurted.

She saw what looked like pity in his eyes, and knew what he must be thinking. She was grasping at straws, deluding herself. He was a man of science and medicine, of cold, hard facts. She wouldn't believe it either, had she been sitting on his side of the desk.

"Please," she said softly.

He scheduled the procedure for later that afternoon.

Twenty minutes later she walked from his office with a handful of prescriptions and more than three hours to kill before her meeting with Tom's lawyer. She got in her Explorer and headed for the plaza, doing her best to ignore the throbbing pain in her head.

Her first stop was at an upscale bed and bath shop. She selected a set of lavender sheets and big, luxurious bath towels in flamboyant shades of purple and pink. She smiled, thinking how much Tom would hate the colors. From the bath shop, she walked next door to a boutique called Pizzazz and bought an outrageously overpriced bottle of jasmine perfume and an equally pricey bottle of bath oil. From there, she drove downtown to her favorite Mexican café for lunch. She swallowed two painkillers with water, ordered a taco salad she was too unnerved to eat, then headed across the street to finish her shopping.

By the time she loaded the last of her purchases into the back of the Explorer, her vision was blurred and her head hurt so badly she thought it would explode. She glanced at her watch. One forty-five. She had fifteen minutes to get across town, and out of Tom's life forever.

The establishment of Geoffrey Blye, Esquire, was a

suite of offices that occupied the upper floor of a large, brick building on Manson Avenue. The scent of leather and expensive cigars greeted Willy as she stepped inside. Her glance moved over the deep, rich carpeting and expertly upholstered furniture. Tom didn't have the kind of money this place was costing. That was for sure. Knowing his parents were picking up the tab for the divorce made Willy feel angry and doubly betrayed.

Tom sat in the waiting area, looking successful and impatient in a charcoal gray suit. He forced a smile and stood to greet Willy when she entered.

"Thanks for coming." He kissed her cheek, and it was all she could do to keep her lunch down. "We can go right in. John's free."

John Blye was a younger version of his father, Geoffrey. He sat behind a desk that looked too large for his thin frame, in an office that looked too imposing for his boyish face. *But he's a snake, just the same,* Willy thought. *Gillian and Thomas Mackenzie would not have hired him, otherwise.*

"Thank you for coming, Tom... Ms. Mackenzie." He shook Tom's hand, barely giving Willy a glance before getting down to business. "Just a few minor details to work out. Shouldn't take long." He leafed through a large, white folder, extracted three documents, and laid them side by side on his desk. He explained them in a legalese that pounded like a jackhammer in Willy's brain. The room was spinning crazily around her. She gripped the arms of her chair, praying she wouldn't be sick. When John Blye finally slid the documents across the desk, she signed all three without reading them. Zoe would probably be furious, but Willy couldn't think about that now. She couldn't think about anything at all.

"Thank you for your time," the lawyer said patronizingly.

Mustering all of the dignity she possessed, Willy stood and walked from the room. Tom caught up with her in the corridor.

"Listen, Willy." He took her arm and steered her to the side of the hallway, standing so close she thought she'd drown in the sweet, pungent odor of his aftershave. "I just wanted to say that I hope in time we can get past this. You know, be friends."

She would have liked to slap him, or at the very least, scream at him, but too ill to do either of those things, she merely nodded.

"I'm sorry for the pain I've caused you, babe. I'm just sorry as hell."

She held it together long enough to reach the ladies room. After she'd thrown up what little lunch she'd eaten, she splashed cool water on her face and took deep, cleansing breaths. *It'll be all right,* she told herself. *Just relax.*

After taking a few moments to compose herself she exited the building and walked to the parking garage. Stepping out of the stairwell, she almost had herself convinced she was all right. She heard the screech of tires as a sleek BMW convertible screamed to stop, mere feet away. A pretty blonde with tanning salon skin and an up-to-the-minute hairstyle sat behind the wheel. Willy stood, frozen in place, as a man in a charcoal gray suit opened the door and slid in beside her. *Tom.*

He gave the girl a kiss and the couple drove away, laughing.

Sadness washed over Willy in waves, as a deep, aching emptiness filled her heart. She was drowning in sorrow and humiliation. All of their years together, their love, meant nothing to him. Nothing at all. She'd once been Tom's prize, but now he'd found a shinier prize, one who made Willy look like a cheap trinket out of a gumball machine. He didn't love her anymore. If he ever loved her at all.

~ * ~

Darby pulled into Willy's driveway, shifted the truck into park, and stared at the empty spot where Willy's Explorer should have been parked. He could hardly contain his disappointment. *Where could she be?*

He sat for a moment, deciding on a plan of action. The biggest part of him wanted to drive home, come back later, when she was here, but his rational mind said that would be a mistake. He had a key to the cottage. He could easily replace the door casings and be gone before Willy returned. After a moment's hesitation, he got out of the truck and lifted the moldings from the bed.

It's just as well, he told himself, not wanting to admit how badly he'd wanted to see her.

He unlocked the back door, fitted in the moldings, and hammered them into place. A faint scent of jasmine drifted out from the kitchen, along with the unmistakable aroma of simmering tomato sauce. Marilyn hadn't been much of a cook. Most of the meals they'd eaten together, Darby had prepared. He thought of the pie Willy had baked for him, pictured her standing at the kitchen counter, doing things with flour and butter, thinking of him. The thought both pleased and angered him.

A bright slip of paper on the kitchen table caught his eye and he walked over to investigate. He picked up the paper, a flyer advertising the third annual Murphy's Crossing Strawberry Festival. A week from Saturday. Willy had circled the date with a magic marker. Darby frowned. He didn't like the idea of Willy spending time in the village. Murphy's Crossing was a small town. People liked to talk. If someone said the wrong thing...

Fighting the urge to crumple the flyer and throw it away, he replaced it on the table and stood, looking around. He liked what she'd done with the place, liked the bouquets of ferns and daisies sitting around in vases, and the basket full of pinecones on the hearth. She liked simple, earthy things. Somehow, that pleased him, too.

Back outside, he gazed at the empty spot in the driveway and frowned again. He didn't like the idea of her spending so much time away from the cottage. Things could happen. Bad things. He locked the door behind him and stepped from the porch, wondering again where she was.

Above his head, a cloud moved across the sun. A chill breeze whispered to him, and he stared down the empty road, as if that would make her materialize.

Where are you, Willy?

Fear crept through his insides, settling in a thick knot in his chest. He'd felt it too many times not to know what it meant. Somewhere, somehow, Willy was in danger.

~ * ~

She was claustrophobic by nature, but today Willy welcomed the chamber's isolation. She lay strapped inside, feeling like Jonah in the belly of the whale, as the machine whirred and clicked, deciding her fate. She lay, breathing in, breathing out, nearly hypnotized by the sound.

An hour later, the radiologist, an older man named Stan, ushered her into his office, a sterile white room filled with tables and high-tech equipment.

"Have a seat, Willow," he said, pulling a chair back from the table.

She sat, hands tightly clasped in her lap, as he entered her data into the computer.

Let it be good news. Oh, Lord... please let it be good news.

Something in Stan's expression as he interpreted the screen made her uneasy.

"All right," he finally said, "these are just the initial findings. Doctor Chan will be able to give you a more thorough interpretation in a day or two, but let's see what we're looking at." His fingers moved across the keyboard and several images filled the screen. There was a dense moment of silence as he stared at them.

"I'm better than I was, aren't I?" she asked, almost a plea.

His glance moved from the screen, to her face, and back again. "No, I'm afraid not."

"I'm not worse, though?"

He sighed.

"I'm worse?"

"Maybe slightly." He worked the keyboard again, and the images he'd shown her a few weeks before lined up beside the new ones. Willy sat, not hearing his explanation, seeing only a cold, gray knot at the base of her skull, a coiled serpent, claiming more and more territory. She stared at the images, fighting tears. "How can that be?"

He laid a gentle hand on her shoulder. "It's not unusual, Willow. I'm sorry if someone's given you false hope. Chemotherapy is not a cure, in your case. Frankly, after one treatment, you shouldn't even be feeling better. The treatments aren't going to cure you, Willow. Only buy you some time."

Driving home, Willy felt as though her head was splitting in two. Tears and dizziness blurred the road ahead as the doctor's words echoed in her mind.

Not better. Worse.

Somehow she made it back to the cottage. She stepped onto the porch, collapsed at the table, and gave in to a torrent of tears she'd thought long spent.

~ * ~

It wasn't just tears. What he was hearing were tearing, gut-wrenching sobs.

Halfway to the porch, Darby stopped in mid-stride. From where he stood in the yard, he could see Willy sitting at the table, her head resting on her arms, crying. If she were to glance up, she would see him, too. He should leave, and quickly, before that happened. He knew that, but somehow, he couldn't.

He stood, indecision cementing his feet firmly in place, until Lucky whined softly, deciding for him. Willy looked up and met his gaze before quickly turning away.

"What do you need, Darby?"

It was the first time she'd addressed him by name, and he felt a curious thrill. He cleared his throat. "I was here earlier and repaired the door moldings. I noticed the lock wasn't working properly. I brought a new one to replace it."

"This isn't a good time."

"Okay." It was time to retreat. She'd made that clear. But the hurting in her eyes made his heart ache. He gazed at her in the gathering shadows, wanting to do something, not knowing what. Lucky whined again, and Willy swiped angrily at her tears with the back of her hand. Darby cleared his throat again. "Are you all right?"

"I'm fine." Her voice broke, and fresh tears spilled down her face.

Darby closed the distance between them in three strides. He came to her side, rested his hand cautiously on her back. "I don't think you are," he said softly.

"Darby, please. Go away." She started to sob again, and he gathered her up in his arms. She resisted for a moment, then rested her head against his chest.

"I saw my husband today," she blurted. "With another woman. A woman with a convertible."

He gently stroked her hair.

"I didn't ever want to see her..." She choked on the words. "I knew there was someone else, but I never wanted to... Oh, God. God damn him."

Anger welled up inside him. "Your husband is a fool," he said, still stroking her hair. "He'll realize that, some day. Some other man will come along, and--"

"There won't be any other man."

"Yes there will. Beautiful woman like you, there will be plenty of men who'll--"

"There won't be any other men, Darby. There won't be time." She added softly, "I'm dying."

He'd known it instinctively. Known it, and not wanted it to be true. Not for Willy. Not when it didn't have to be. A voice raged in his head, telling him to retreat, to let nature take its course. He struggled with it, indecision festering like a fever in his brain. She buried her face in his chest, all of the fight gone out of her. In that instant, his decision was made.

"You'll be all right," he said softly.

She shook her head. "No, I won't."

He tilted her tear stained face to meet his. "Yes, you will."

"How do you know?"

"Because I know."

All of time seemed to stop as he gazed into her eyes. Beautiful, sad eyes. Her pretty pink lips parted. "How do you know, Darby?" she whispered.

A voice raged inside his head. *Retreat!* It would be the right thing to do, the safe thing. He couldn't. All he could do was savor the sweetness, the softness of her, as he gently brought his lips down to meet hers.

Eight

His kiss was powerful, and yet, tender. Giving, and at the same time, demanding.

Never in her life had Willy received such a kiss. She yielded to Darby's rock-solid strength, as helpless as a child. Never had she felt more safe, or more vulnerable. She was lost in this man, this stormy, sensitive man, who had three times reached out to cushion her fall. Twice physically, and now emotionally. His mouth covered hers, bruising, and yet... healing. Even now, the pain was leaving her body, slipping away into the past like a bad memory.

"Willy," he whispered, his hands finding their way beneath her jacket, "Sweet Willy."

She ached with pleasure as his hands crept inside her bra and caressed her breasts. She melted against him, wanting more of him. Wanting all of him.

Willy, stop! You don't even know this man! The voice of reason shrieked in her head, shattering the moment and she firmly pushed him away.

"I'm sorry, Darby. I can't do this."

He released her slowly, reluctantly.

"It's not that I'm not attracted to you. I am. It's--"

"It's me who should apologize, Willy. I was out of line. I--" He blew out a deep breath and raked his hands back through his hair. "I should go."

"Yeah. Maybe you should."

She watched him walk away. He was halfway across the yard, when she suddenly felt terrified at the thought of being alone. "Darby, wait," she called softly.

He turned back.

"I don't want you to go." She took a step toward him. "What I mean is, we don't have to... I mean, if you stay... we could talk awhile. If you want to. Have you eaten?"

"No."

"I made spaghetti. We could eat."

He was struggling with the idea. She could see it in his eyes, in his stance, turned half toward her and half away.

"Please?"

In the kitchen, the pot of sauce simmered tantalizingly on the stove and Willy was glad she'd thought to make it. "I just have to boil the pasta," she told him. "And make a salad. It'll only take a minute."

"No hurry."

She went to the cupboard, retrieved a bottle of wine and two glasses, and set them on the counter. She opened the bottle, filled one of the glasses, and handed it to him. "Sit down and relax while I set the table."

"You sit down and relax," he said, handing the glass back to her. "I can set the table." He opened a cupboard and inspected its contents. "Where do you keep your plates?"

"I threw them away." Seeing his puzzled expression, she explained, "Well, I didn't throw them away, exactly. I gave them to the church."

"Oh."

"It's a long story. I've got a new set out in the truck."

While she sliced tomatoes for a salad, Darby went outside and retrieved the shopping bags from the Explorer. Back in the kitchen, he unboxed the dishes, filled the sink with water, and began to wash them.

"You're good at that," Willy commented. "A lot of men wouldn't know the first thing."

Darby shrugged. "Man lives alone long enough, he learns things."

"I guess the same could be said for a woman. Has it been a long time... for you?"

"Yep." He dried the plates and arranged them on the table, pulled two napkins from a nearby stack and set them beside the plates. He added silverware, then, almost as an afterthought, lit the candle in the center of the table.

Moments later, Willy set a steaming bowl of pasta and a crisp salad between the two plates. Her glance moved over him as he piled his dinner plate with spaghetti. He was a big man. Much bigger than Tom. It had been a long time since she'd had dinner with a man and a small thrill rippled through her as she slid into the chair opposite him.

They ate in silence for a time, then Darby startled her by asking, "Do you want to talk about what happened today?"

"What?"

"Your husband. Do you want to talk about it?"

"Oh. No."

"Okay."

She swallowed a forkful of spaghetti, then another. "It's just... so difficult. To give someone so much of yourself and then one day wake up and realize that you're not needed any more. That you've been thrown away."

His eyes held hers, and Willy had never felt more heard, more understood. Tom used to tune her out. She would see his eyes slide away as she spoke and know his interest had waned, as though her thoughts had no value whatsoever. Darby, on the other hand, seemed to digest every word she said. He was a complex and intriguing man, she realized, a man of secrets. Willy found herself wanting to know them all.

"Were you ever married, Darby?"

"I came close once. Didn't work out."

"No?"

"No."

Seeing he wasn't going to elaborate, she tried another path. "Did you grow up in Murphy's Crossing?"

"West Dover. It's a couple of towns over."

"Do your folks still live there?"

"I don't have any folks, Willy. I was raised by the county."

"Orphaned?"

"Thrown away."

"Your parents put you in foster care?" Willy shuddered, remembering her grandmother's constant threats, her terrifying accounts of the life Willy would be given over to if she didn't tow the line.

"It was a farm," Darby told her. "Run by the county. For kids who had nowhere else to be."

"Sounds lonely."

He shrugged. "I survived."

"Still..."

"I had a roof over my head. Three meals a day. And that dog," he gestured to Lucky, who lay in the corner.

"You're kidding!"

"They brought him to the farm when I was twelve. He was a Christmas gift to all of us, but he seemed to love me the most. Hell, maybe he knew I needed him the most."

"Good Lord, how old is Lucky? Around eighteen?"

"Something like that."

He picked up the bottle of wine, topped off their glasses, took a swallow. "This is good."

She took a swallow from her glass, carefully steering the conversation back to him. "You had your grandfather, though, right? You and he must have kept in contact."

"You ask a lot of questions."

"Does that bother you?"

"What's past is past, Willy. It's best to leave it alone."

~ * ~

It surprised him how easily he shared himself with Willy, how he gave her so freely the information Marilyn had had to coax and cajole and, finally, wrench out of him. But Willy was different from Marilyn. She was different from any woman he'd ever known.

Having grown up the only daughter of a wealthy Manhattan attorney, Marilyn had always had more money than good sense. She'd stumbled upon the cottage in her twenty-fifth summer, a gifted painter seeking a quiet and beautiful place in which to create her art. She was spoiled and headstrong, used to getting what she wanted. She decided early on that she wanted Darby. He'd known from the start it wasn't a good match, but blinded by her stunning good looks and her charismatic charm, he was powerless to resist.

He chanced another glance into Willy's eyes. She was a different sort of beautiful. She had a sweet, gentle nature and a dark, sorrowful side he suspected she rarely showed the world. She was damned easy to talk to and he found himself wishing he could sit right there at her table and talk to her for the rest of his life. Still, he'd have to be careful, ease her into the truth. Eventually he'd have to tell her all of it. But not tonight.

When they finished their dinner, Willy got busy clearing away the plates. She piled them in the sink and returned to the table with two cups of coffee. The advertisement was still sitting where he'd left it and she grabbed it up and set it down in front of him. "What do you know about this festival?" she asked.

He shrugged. "There's not much to know. It's a hokey little festival that was designed to bring people to Murphy's Crossing to spend their money. Mostly, it just gives the ladies of the Women's Auxiliary something to fuss about."

Willy smiled. "Wanna go?"

"No."

"They're selling hot air balloon rides," she coaxed.

"Why would you want to ride in a hot air balloon?"

"I've always wanted to ride in a hot air balloon. Go with me?"

"No."

"Why not?"

"It doesn't interest me, Willy."

"You're scared."

He gazed at her for a long moment then let his eyes drop away. *Scared as hell, darlin'.* "No. I'm practical."

She sighed. "Then I guess I'll have to go alone."

"Let me know how it works out for you."

She folded the flyer and set it aside.

"Where did you get that, anyway?" he asked, gesturing toward the flyer.

"The farmer's wife gave it to me when I went to buy flowers. Oh, that reminds me, James Weatherby sends his regards."

He'd been about to swallow a mouthful of coffee and nearly choked on it. "What?"

"James Weatherby said to say hello. To your grandfather."

"Who is he?"

"Just an old man he used to ride to work with."

Darby struggled to keep a passive face as his mind worked on the information. He wouldn't have thought there were many left who remembered. Evidently he'd thought wrong. James Weatherby. One more good reason to discourage Willy from hanging out in town.

"I'll mention it to him," he said. "More coffee?"

"It's a gorgeous night," Willy said. "Let's sit outside."

They carried their cups to the porch and sat at the table, talking softly until the last trace of daylight slipped away. Willy gave him an abbreviated account of her marriage and her recent diagnosis with a malignant brain tumor. When she steered the conversation back to him, Darby stood to leave.

"You've had a big day. I should go, let you get some rest. I'll see you in the morning."

"You will?" she asked.

"I still want to replace that lock."

"Oh."

He hesitated, wanting to kiss her again, not knowing whether it was appropriate.

"Good night, then."

She stood on tiptoe and softly kissed his cheek. "Thanks, Darby."

"For what?"

"For being a friend when I needed one. I won't forget it."

He looked into her eyes, her beautiful eyes. "Goodnight, Willy."

She smiled. "Goodnight."

He felt her eyes on his back as he walked away. He was almost to his truck before he turned back. She stood on the porch, a fragile silhouette in the moonlight. A dream. "Hey, Willy?"

"Yes?"

"The festival... the hot air balloon ride? I'll think about it, okay?"

"Okay," she said softly.

Somewhere in the darkness, he felt her smile.

~ * ~

Willy lay awake for a long time that night. She stared at the ceiling, playing the day's events over in her mind. It seemed like a year had passed since she got out of bed that morning. So many things had changed. The memory of Tom and his lover was painful, and the implications of the MRI, terrifying, so she allowed her thoughts to linger on Darby instead.

She shivered, remembering the thrill of his lips on hers, the sheer comfort of his arms locked around her. She couldn't stop hearing his voice, or remembering his eyes, and the way they seemed to swallow her up. She'd started dating at age sixteen, had been married for five years, and yet, she couldn't remember ever feeling more connected to a man than now. Certainly she had never felt this in-tune with Tom.

She rolled over and stared up at the moon. Tom had never understood her, never even tried, but Darby... Darby knew where she was coming from because he'd been there, too. He knew how it felt to grow up poor and unwanted. *Thrown away.*

She thought about that for a moment.

Something he'd said troubled her, some vague idea that seemed just out of reach. She stared at the moon as if it held the answer, going over their conversation again and again in her mind. Finally, too exhausted to think about it anymore, she tumbled off to sleep.

Nine

Darby lay wide awake in the dark with his senses on red alert. He couldn't stop thinking about Willy and how alive she made him feel. He thought of her eyes and her hands and the sweet taste of her lips, and his heart overflowed. He thought of the pieces of her past she'd shared with him. She hadn't had an easy time of it and with everything inside of him, he longed to make it up to her, to travel life's road by her side, celebrating the good times and easing the sting of the bad. But would she allow him to share her life if she knew the truth?

He studied the situation from every angle, anticipating every possible outcome. They were two desperate people, each clinging to their existence by a fragile thread. He could offer her his love, but would love be enough?

In the best scenarios she accepted him for what he was and returned his love, but in the worst, she fled from him in horror. Those torturing thoughts kept him tossing and turning.

He lay awake for hours, battling with his feelings and struggling to keep his memories at bay. Somewhere in the night they crashed past his defenses, like a raging current, pulling him back in time, back to the source of his fears.

Back to Marilyn...

~ * ~

The storm seemed to have come from out of nowhere. Lightning blazed a path across the sky, while thunder shook the walls of the cabin. Marilyn lay in his bed, soft and warm beside him. He held her close to his heart, like the treasure she was. He'd thought her asleep until she turned and her voice became a whisper in his ear.

"Darby, are you awake?"

"Yeah."

"I've got a secret."

He studied her face in the shadows. She was smiling, a small, mysterious, woman-smile. He braced himself, wondering whether it was one of her games: another secret divulged in order to coax one out of him.

"Tell me."

She smiled again, wider now. She uttered a pair of words, and suddenly, nothing was the same.

Hours later, when the sun began to bruise the morning sky and the torrent of rainfall tapered off to a light mist, she dropped off to sleep, exhausted and exasperated.

They'd talked all night, resolving nothing. He left her in his bed and went out for a drive, hoping it would clear his head, hoping it would calm the fear that raged inside him.

It wasn't that he was unhappy about the baby. All his life Darby had dreamed of having a child. His own child, to teach and to guide... to love. It was a dream he'd given up on, and now, staring into the face of it, he was consumed by the sheer wanting of it, the impossibility of it. No, he wasn't unhappy about the baby. The baby was right.

It was the timing that was wrong.

Already Marilyn was talking about returning to New York City, talking about opportunities and advantages. She'd offered Darby a compromise: they'd buy an apartment in Soho in which to live, and spend their summers in Baker's Gully. The child would have the best of both worlds. When he hedged, she became angry and frustrated. She saw his staunch refusal to leave Murphy's Crossing as bull-headedness, as something that would have to be worked out. But there was no way to work it out. He knew that with every breath in his body. He couldn't go to New York City. He couldn't go anywhere at all.

He rounded a sharp bend and hit the brakes hard. A maple tree had fallen across the road. Struck by lightning, he judged, considering the jagged stump. He eased around it, making a mental note to call the highway department from town and let them know about it.

The village streets were wet and the misting rain cast hazy prisms beneath the streetlamps. Darby stopped at the general store, bought eggs and cheese, a gigantic bouquet of flowers. He'd make the day a celebration. He'd shower Marilyn with love, convince her to raise the child in Baker's Gully. He'd reach deep down inside himself, and somehow find the words to tell her the truth. He'd make her see how beautiful and magical their life would be. Driving home, he'd almost convinced himself it was possible.

Back at the cabin, he put the bouquet in a glass of water. He cracked open a half dozen eggs in a fry pan, grated some of the cheese he bought and threw it in with the eggs. When they were cooked through, he turned down the flame and went to wake Marilyn.

He found the bed empty, her nightgown lying in a heap on the floor. Across the room, the closet door was ajar. He pushed it open, fear snaking through his insides, hissing of danger. His strong box lay open on the closet floor. The lock had been smashed, its broken pieces left in a twisted *pile beside the box. She'd removed his papers, strewn them haphazardly across the floor: his Army records, a handful of photographs, his birth certificate.*

Fear slammed through his veins as he raced outside to his truck, threw it in gear, and drove across the river to the cottage.

He found Marilyn in the bedroom. Her suitcases lay open on the bed, as she hurriedly threw things in. He said her name and she looked at him, her eyes wide, wild. He saw fear in them. Fear and something else. Something that looked an awful lot like revulsion.

"Marilyn..."

"What are you?"

His throat was parched, his heart, pounding. He took a step toward her. "I'm a man, Marilyn. A man that loves you more than life."

He reached out, softly touched her cheek.

She recoiled. "Don't touch me!"

"Marilyn, please. Please let me explain it to you."

She shook her head. Her eyes darted across the room, seeking an escape.

"You owe me that much," he pleaded, reaching out to her again.

She reached inside the suitcase. When her hand reappeared, he saw it held a gun.

"There's nothing you can say, Darby. Nothing I want to hear." She pointed the gun steadily at his face. "I'm leaving here now. And whoever... whatever you are, if you try and stop me I'll kill you." With the gun aimed at his face, she picked up the suitcase and backed from the room.

He stepped in front of her, blocking the doorway. "You'll have to shoot me, then, Marilyn, because I'm not letting you leave until you've heard me out. Now put the suitcase down."

The gun trembled in her hand. "Get out of my way,

Darby."

He reached out to her again. "Give me the gun."
She shook her head.
"Marilyn."
She closed her eyes and fired three bullets into his chest.

~ * ~

He staggered out to the woods and collapsed on a blanket of pine needles. For four days, Lucky remained at his side. When he awoke on the fifth day, Marilyn was nothing more than a rumor.

Stories of her untimely death were passed over the counter at the hardware store, whispered about over steaming cups of coffee at the Four Leaf Clover Diner. She had become a tragic heroine, a fairy tale gone awry. They talked about the mysterious, beautiful young artist, speeding down Baker's Gully in the rain. The townspeople came up with a dozen different scenarios during the first year after her death, a dozen different ways to talk about her. After the second year, they didn't talk about her at all.

In the end only one truth remained. She'd been driving fast on wet roads, slammed into a fallen tree at sixty miles per hour and sent her car toppling end over end. In the end only one truth mattered. She was gone and it was all his fault. Marilyn. His Marilyn...

On the sixth day he'd packed up her things and stowed them in the attic. On the seventh day he closed up the cottage, along with his heart, vowing never to open either one again.

He lay in the dark with tears streaming down his face and his heart an open wound. He thought again of Willy's kiss, and her eyes, and her smile, and an aching went straight through his soul. The truth might drive her away, as it had Marilyn, but that was a chance he'd have to take. For better or for worse, and for the last time in his life, he was in love.

Ten

The trilling of birds and the gentle shushing sounds of the river drifted in through the open window, pulling Willy from her dreams. She lingered in bed for a moment, savoring the quiet noises of the valley and wondering what the day would bring. Her thoughts drifted back to Darby and the puzzle she'd been working on before falling asleep. What was it he'd said that bothered her so? Still unable to grasp hold of it, she pushed back the sheets and tumbled out of bed. He'd said he'd be there early to replace the lock. She certainly didn't want to be lounging in bed when he arrived.

She padded out to the kitchen and made a pot of coffee, then wandered to the window. The river sparkled in the morning sunshine and the wildflowers stood tall and proud and bright with dew. Her gaze was drawn across the water, to Darby's cabin. She thought again of his kiss, and a small thrill shivered through her.

Willy, stop setting yourself up for disappointment! her voice of reason scolded. *It probably didn't mean anything to him at all.* She tucked her robe closer around her and went to take a shower, not wanting to admit how eager she was to see him again.

When she returned to the kitchen, twenty minutes later, the coffee's rich, aromatic scent filled the house. She'd just poured her first cup when she heard a soft knock at the door. She hurried to answer it, cursing the butterflies that fluttered in her stomach.

Darby stood on the porch, looking like the answer to some sort of prayer. His hair was damp from the shower, last night's beard stubble shaved clean. She saw his eyes move over her, and the raw appreciation they held made her tingle.

"Good morning," he said.

"Good morning, Darby."

"I hope I'm not too early."

"Actually you're right on time. I was just about to make breakfast."

While Darby went to work on the lock, Willy returned to the kitchen and assembled the ingredients for pancakes. It had seemed awkward, yesterday, having a man at her table, but in the light of a brand new day it felt right, natural somehow, to be sharing a meal with him.

With the lock replaced, Darby came inside to wash his hands. Willy flipped a stack of steaming pancakes onto a platter and carried them to the table. They talked about the weather and the family of mallards that had made their nest in the reeds along the riverbank. Willy had always been shy, especially around men, and was surprised by the easy give and take of their conversation.

"The temperature's supposed to reach ninety by the weekend," he commented.

"Well, at least it isn't supposed to rain." She took a swallow of coffee, not meeting his eyes. "That would spoil our balloon ride."

A hint of a smile played at his lips. "*Our* balloon ride?"

"Well... yeah."

He drained his coffee cup and set it back on the table. "I don't remember saying I'd go."

"You said you'd think about it."

"I did think about it."

"And?"

"And I've come up with a proposition."

"Oh?"

"*If* I go to the festival with you, then you've got to do something for me."

Her heart jolted inside her. "Like what?"

"Like make me another apple pie. It's my favorite."

She grinned. "Done."

"And..."

"And?"

"Help me clip Lucky's toenails."

"Ick."

"I'll do the clipping. You just have to distract him while I do it."

She sighed. "Okay, I guess that's easy enough."

"*And* I wouldn't mind having some more of these pancakes again sometime."

"Darby, that's three things."

"So far."

"You're impossible."

"Not impossible, Sis," he said with a wink. "Just difficult."

She felt her face flush with pleasure. "You really liked the pancakes, then?"

"I loved the pancakes."

"Next time I'll make them with berries, if you'll let me pick from the bushes on the path."

"Help yourself."

"Would you come with me? You and Lucky... just in case?"

An hour later they were tramping through the woods. Willy was disappointed to discover the berry patch on the path picked clean, but Darby said he knew of another patch, deeper in the woods. After hiking another mile, they reached a clearing bordered by thick tangles of bushes. "Will that be enough berries for you?" he asked.

"Hot dog!" Willy exclaimed. "Looks like the three bears haven't discovered this part of the woods yet."

"Well then you'd better get busy, Goldilocks, before they do."

They talked easily as they filled their buckets until the conversation faded into comfortable silence. With his bucket filled, Darby picked up a large stick and threw it into the meadow. Lucky bounded through the tall grass, retrieved it, and brought it back. Willy watched them play, a sense of well being swelling inside her. The sun picked up the copper strands in Darby's hair, making it shine like a gleaming penny. *That is one beautiful man,* she thought. He fit perfectly here, as much a part of the landscape as the towering oaks or the endless blue sky. All at once she was consumed by the desire to belong to him, to be a part of his world, for as long as forever lasted.

He glanced up and saw her staring. "All set?"

"I think so," she said, quickly recovering.

He grabbed up the buckets and carried them back through the woods. When they reached the river, he set them down on the bank. "Care to go for a swim?"

"I don't have a suit."

He grinned. "I don't mind."

"I do."

"Suit yourself." He rolled his jeans to his knees and waded out into the water.

"Wait for me!" Willy rolled up her jeans and waded in behind him. The water felt cool and refreshing against her skin and she contemplated swimming in her clothes. As she stepped deeper into the river, something large brushed against her leg. She yelped and scrambled back to the riverbank. "Oh my God! There's something *huge* in there!"

"Do you suppose it's a shark?" Darby said, clearly

hiding a smile.

"I'm not kidding, Darby. Something just brushed against my leg. Something big!"

He didn't try to hide his laughter. "It was probably a trout, Willy. This river is full of them." He held out his hand. "Come back."

She took a cautious step toward him. "Do they bite?"

"Nothing but the end of a fish hook, darlin'. Come on."

They splashed in the river for most of the afternoon. When the sun began to set they returned to Darby's cabin. Willy sat on the porch while Darby prepared two tall glasses of sweet tea.

They sat in the waning daylight, enjoying each other's company and the cool, sweet liquid. It was one of the nicest days Willy could remember.

Her hair felt wet and heavy against her neck, and she scooped it up in her hands to take advantage of the cooling breeze that whispered through the pines.

"What have you got there?" Darby asked, his hand lightly brushing the spot between her shoulder blades. "A tattoo?"

"My friend, Sid, is a tattoo artist. I let her practice on me, back when she was apprenticing."

"It's very good," he said, studying the artwork. "Intricate."

"Thank you."

"A dove with a broken wing." His eyes sought hers, questioning, and she quickly looked away as a moment from her childhood came flooding back. The memory was painful, and not something easily shared. Darby's hand moved to her cheek and brushed away a stray tear. "What is it, Willy? What's inside that's hurting you so?"

She was afraid of the compassion and the naked desire she saw in his eyes, afraid of the feelings she knew were all too obvious in her own and so she fled, giving him a flimsy excuse about having laundry to do. Halfway down the path she wished she'd stayed, knowing that every moment away would be a moment spent wishing she were with him.

Eleven

Darby stood waist-deep in the river, watching as Willy waded out to him. She wore a pair of cut-off blue jeans, a tank top, and a pair of his old fishing boots. She had never looked more beautiful, her hair shimmering in the sunshine, her skin as luscious as a golden peach.

"I'm glad you changed your mind about tomorrow, Darby," she said. "I really didn't want to go to the festival alone." She smiled at him, nearly taking his breath away; no idea how magnificent she was, no idea that he would have gladly crawled to the top of Mt. Everest if she'd asked him to.

Tearing his eyes from her, he shrugged. "It won't kill me."

"Still, I know you didn't really want to go and I appreciate it."

He shrugged again.

"Did I tell you we have to be there at five o'clock?"

"Five o'clock in the morning?"

"I guess I forgot to mention it."

"Yeah, I guess you did."

"Five o'clock is the first launch. It was the only time

slot I could get on such short notice."

He rolled his eyes. "Swell."

She bit her lip. "I'm sorry."

"I'm only kidding with you, Willy. Hell, back when I was in the army I'd already put in a half a day by five."

She reached his side and he handed her a fishing pole and a large metal bucket. "There's a sink hole just around the bend. I usually have pretty good luck there."

"I didn't know you were in the Army."

"It was a long time ago." He slung his pole over his shoulder and slogged a path through the water, Willy following closely behind him. When they reached the fishing hole, he indicated a large, flat rock. "Best seat in the house."

As Willy perched on the edge of the rock, Darby opened his tackle box, removed a grub, and threaded it onto her hook. He handed her the fishing pole. "Do you know how to cast your line?"

"Not a clue."

He reached for the pole, but she stubbornly held it out of his reach. "I'll figure it out. How hard can it be?"

~ * ~

He watched as she clumsily slung the line over her shoulder. As she thrust the pole forward, the hook sailed through the air, neatly snagging his shirt.

"Hey, lady! Watch what you're doing."

"Oh, Darby, I'm so sorry!" Her laughter rang out across the valley, filling him with joy.

He removed the hook from his shirt, cast her line in the water, and handed her back the pole. "We're supposed to be quiet," he told her in an exaggerated whisper.

"I'm sorry," she whispered, tempering her laughter.

They sat together in companionable silence while butterflies danced in the sun- kissed morning and Lucky chased chipmunks along the riverbank. Darby watched Willy from the corner of his eye, savoring her beauty and her gentle spirit, trying to ignore the desire she stirred deep inside him.

"It's so beautiful here," Willy murmured. "Have you lived here long?"

He tensed slightly. "Long enough."

She regarded him thoughtfully. "You don't ever give a straight answer, do you?"

He sighed. "Long enough that I could never go back to living in town. How's that?"

"It'll do."

A smile played at the corners of her mouth, and Darby slowly relaxed. There were so many things he wanted to tell her, so many parts of himself he longed to share, but he didn't know whether he had the courage. Getting involved with her would be asking for heartache. Hell, it would be begging for it.

"Darby," she whispered excitedly, "I think I've got one."

Seeing her line stretched taut, he took the fishing pole from her and slowly reeled it in. When she saw the oversized trout on the end of her line she squealed like a child.

"I can't believe I made the first catch!"

He removed the fish from her line and dropped it in the bucket. "Not bad. For a beginner."

"What do you mean, not bad? That is one gorgeous fish!"

As she leaned over to examine her catch, Darby caught a glimpse down the front of her shirt. She had on some sort of fancy brassiere: a lacy, black thing that hugged her perfect breasts and nearly made him salivate. Desire pounded through his veins, and he turned his eyes away, not wanting her to see how badly he wanted to make love to her.

~ * ~

She didn't know him, but oh, how she wanted him.

She wanted his strength and his quiet laughter. She wanted his arms wrapped tightly around her, his mouth pressed against hers. Darby Sullivan was everything a man should be, and she ached to lie down beside him, to experience the power and the wonder of him. She ached to know his secrets, and to share her secrets with him.

She tore her eyes away from him, feeling naked and vulnerable. She'd never been so fiercely attracted to a man. Not even Tom had stirred her like this. She gazed into the river, unable to fathom how it had come about, how she could have given her heart away so quickly.

"What are you thinking about, Willy?" He asked, breaking into her thoughts.

"Nothing."

"Must be something, to have put that far away look in your eyes."

"I was thinking about my grandmother," she blurted.

"Your grandmother?"

It was the last thing she meant to tell him. She never told anyone about the dove, except Sid. But now that she'd started, she had no choice but to see it through.

"She had a boyfriend, when I was growing up. Actually, she had a lot of them." She gazed into the water, gathering the courage to continue. "But there was this one man, this truck driver named Buss. I hated him the most."

He watched her intently, waiting.

"He took us to Florida when I was ten. My grandmother had never seen the ocean and she begged Buss to take her over-the-road. She tried for days to find someone to leave me with but there were no takers, so they had to drag me along. She wasn't happy about it. Neither was Buss, for that matter."

A long moment passed as Darby waited for her to continue. "I fell head over heels in love with the ocean--the swell of the waves, the call of the seagulls. I'd never experienced anything so wonderful. I wanted to stay there forever. We drove a thousand miles, and Buss said I had one hour to look around. I spent the hour splashing in the waves and exploring. I found all of the usual treasures: sea glass, a handful of shells. And then I found a sand dollar. I didn't know what it was, but I thought it was the most beautiful thing I had ever seen. I hid it in my shirt."

"Why?" he asked softly.

"Because I knew she'd take it away from me."

She sat for a moment, lost in the memory.

"When the hour was up, Eva made me throw the seashells back in the ocean, just like I knew she would."

"Why did she make you throw them away?"

"I wasn't allowed to have anything beautiful, Darby. Not forever. Just long enough to know the pain of losing." The memory was painful, powerful. She felt tears gathering in her eyes and blinked them back.

"Buss was hungry, so we left the beach and drove to a seafood restaurant. I stumbled while I was trying to climb out of the truck, and the sand dollar fell out of my shirt. I scrambled to pick it up, but Buss got his hands on it first. I begged him to give it back to me. Instead he put it down his pants and told me I'd have to come and get it. He laughed like it was the funniest thing in the world.

"Of course, Eva was furious. She demanded that he give her the sand dollar. When he did, she threw it on the ground and stepped on it, grinding it under her heel. Then she hit me in the face, screaming about what a tramp I was, and how she didn't want to be seen in public with me." Tears flowed, unchecked, down her face. "They left me out in the parking lot and went inside the restaurant. As soon as they were gone I picked through the pieces of my beautiful sand dollar, and I found a tiny white dove. Its wing was broken, but other than that, it had survived Eva's cruelty. Somehow, that dove came to define me."

His hand crept across the distance between them, until it found hers and swallowed it up. "I'm sorry, Willy."

She wiped her tears with the hankie he offered. "It was a long time ago. Like you said, a person should learn to leave the past alone."

~ * ~

Tired of chasing chipmunks, Lucky swam out to where they sat. He climbed onto the rock next to Willy and shook himself off, showering her with water and lightening her mood. Their conversation turned to Murphy's Crossing, and what Darby knew of its rich, Irish history.

As the noon whistle echoed in the distance, Darby dropped the last catch of the day into the bucket and stood. "I think we're all set. Looks like we've got enough fish to feed the town."

"So now we get to eat them, right?"

"Yep. Just as soon as we clean them."

She made a face and he reached for the bucket. "Better let me carry that."

"Don't be silly, Darby. You've got all the other stuff. I can get it."

"You sure? It's mighty heavy."

"Yes, I'm sure." She stubbornly clung to the bucket. "I'm not as helpless as you seem to think I am."

They plodded back through the water, Willy struggling with the bucket.

"I wish you'd let me carry that," he grumbled. "You're going to drop it, and there goes our lunch."

"No, I'm not."

He cursed her stubborn streak and climbed onto the riverbank as Willy crept across on stepping stones. Almost to the bank, she set her foot down on a turtle that hid among the large, flat rocks.

"Watch out," he cautioned. "You don't want to step on that--"

The turtle poked its head out from beneath its shell, startling her, and she stumbled backward, dropping the bucket. She made a grab for it, but by then, the trout were swimming away down stream.

"Oh, no!" she wailed.

The expression on her mud-streaked face was priceless, and Darby bit back a smile. "Are you all right?"

"Yes, I'm all right, but... but all our beautiful fish..." Rising to her feet, she gazed wistfully in the direction of the departing fish. She lost her footing, stumbling again.

He waded toward her. "Let me give you a hand there, Grace."

"That's not a bit funny."

"It's a little bit funny," he said, extending his hand.

~ * ~

She was quick; he had to give her that. Before he saw it coming, she pulled the bucket up out of the water and doused him full in the face.

"Now *that's* funny!"

Her laughter rang out in the silent afternoon as she got to her feet and scrambled toward the bank.

"Oh, this means war!" he shouted, hurrying after her. Lucky barked joyously from the bank as Darby pursued her. Within moments, he tackled her. His arms went around her waist, pulling her down into the water.

They both came up, laughing, gasping for breath. His arms were still around her, his face, inches from hers. "Now you're my prisoner," he said huskily. Then his lips were on hers, his tongue probing the sweetness of her mouth. Desire consumed him as her body melted against his. His kiss went deeper, as he held her tighter, wanting to take her inside himself, to erase the hurt, to fill her with his love. He couldn't change her past any more than he could change his own. But maybe together they could go forward.

Thoughts of Marilyn intruded, shattering the

moment. Marilyn had found out the truth and hated him for it. The memory of that jagged, aching pain forced him to end the kiss. One day, he would take Willy to his bed. *After* she knew the truth, and if she still wanted him.

She rested her head on chest. "Are you mad at me?"

"No."

"I let our fish get away."

"There are more fish in the sea, Willy. Didn't anyone ever tell you that?"

She looked up into his eyes, held them for a long moment. "It'll take a lot of work."

"I'm willing to give it a try. If you are."

"We'd have to start all over again."

He pulled her closer to his chest, stroked her hair. "Then that's what we do, Willy. We start all over again."

Twelve

It was a damned fool idea and he wished he'd never agreed to it.

Darby pulled his truck into the large, empty field adjacent to the Murphy's Crossing Fire Department, where a handmade sign announced: Festival Parking $2.

He pulled up beside a makeshift booth, letting the truck idle.

"I don't think there's anyone here to take the money," Willy said.

"Doesn't look it." He let the truck idle for a moment more then drove past the booth and into a rutted pasture. He drove to where a handful of cars were clustered together at the edge of the field, parked the truck, and got out. The first rays of sunlight had just begun to pierce the sky, and the morning had an eerie, peaceful quality about it.

"Looks like they're setting up over there." Willy pointed to a wide-open expanse of land that had been roped off beyond the parking area. Darby could see a half dozen brightly painted trailers, crews of men and women scurrying about amid the various equipment. The low roar of a propane flame igniting shattered the quiet as a blue and gold balloon rose gracefully into the sky.

"Oh my God, Darby, can you believe we're actually

doing this?" There was no mistaking the excitement in Willy's voice, or the sparkle in her eyes. Not wanting to dampen her enthusiasm, Darby forced a smile as they hurried toward the assemblage. There weren't many things in life he was afraid of, but hovering thousands of feet above the earth in a wicker basket suspended from a balloon definitely topped the list.

Willy scanned the trailers, which were painted in bold colors and bearing names like Purple Cloud, and Golden Eternity. "We're looking for the Blue Haze."

"I feel like I'm in a blue haze," he muttered.

She stopped walking and stared at him. "Are you grumpy?"

"No, I'm not grumpy. I just want to get this over with."

They passed the next three work crews and finally came to a pale blue trailer with swirling violet letters that proudly identified itself as The Blue Haze.

"Here it is!" Willy said, making a grab for his hand.

The Blue Haze was spread out on the ground, six men surrounding it, working furiously to prepare it for flight. The sight of the balloon caused a fist to squeeze in Darby's gut. One hundred feet of blue nylon and a white wicker basket that for the next hour would hold his fate. Good God, what was he thinking?

Willy watched as if mesmerized while the pilot prepared to inflate the balloon. He lit a torch. The roar of the burner was almost deafening as slowly, the Blue Haze began to rise. It floated majestically in the air above the basket, a gentle giant, and despite himself, Darby was impressed.

The pilot, an unkempt man of approximately sixty, grinned widely, exposing the evidence of decades of poor oral hygiene.

"Wa-Hoo!" he shouted raucously. "Let's getter done!"

He instructed Willy to climb into the basket, pointing out the foot holes in the side. When he had guided her in, he turned expectantly to Darby.

The basket was divided into three compartments, and Darby swung his legs over the side and into the last empty compartment. The pilot recited a list of safety instructions before once again displaying his rotted teeth. He slapped Darby on the back. "Main thing is, let's have some fun!"

Perfect, Darby thought glumly. *A million hot air balloonists in the world, and I get stuck with Larry the Cable Guy.*

The pilot opened a valve on a second propane tank and its flame shot up into the center of the balloon. Willy grabbed Darby's hand, squeezing it tightly as the balloon slowly climbed into the sky. It was an odd sensation, and not like anything Darby had ever experienced. It wasn't a sense of climbing, as much as one of the earth falling away. The pilot radioed his crew, and they answered him in a crackle of static. It wasn't like any code Darby ever heard and he soon lost interest in trying to decipher it.

"How far are we going?" Willy asked the pilot.

"Oh, ten, twelve miles, I expect."

"So that will put us in Ossian, if we go south. Or close to Nunda, if we go east?"

"Can't guarantee where we'll end up, Missy. Whichever way the wind blows is where she'll take us. She don't come equipped with a steering wheel." The man affectionately patted the basket.

Willy listened with rapt attention as the pilot related stories of the places he'd been and the things he'd seen in his balloon. Darby let the pilot's voice fade away, focusing his attention on the spectacular view. The morning was clear and cool, and the air, fresher than any he had ever breathed. From this vantage point he could see the entire valley. He gazed down at the panorama of farmland and forest, and directly beneath him, at the village of Murphy's Crossing. Tiny people moved around in streets bordered by miniature buildings. It was as though he were God, except he had no control over his own destiny, at the moment, let alone the tiny people below him.

After they'd gone a mile or more, even the pilot fell silent, as if he, too was overwhelmed by the view. Darby felt the squeeze of Willy's hand in his, and glancing over, saw that her attention was focused not on the valley below, but on the clouds.

"What do you think is out there, Darby?" she whispered.

His slid his arm around her waist, pulling her as close as the partition would allow. "People have been asking that question for thousands of years, darlin'," he said.

"It doesn't seem as though it could be anything bad, does it?"

He gave her another squeeze and said nothing.

An hour and fifteen minutes later, the pilot landed the balloon in a field eleven miles away. The chase crew had been trailing in their vehicles and arrived within moments after the landing. Five crew members and the pilot fussed over the balloon, and within a half hour, the Blue Haze was safely back in its trailer, and he and Willy were being chauffeured to town in a Dodge Ram pickup.

When they reached Murphy's Crossing it was after eight, and the village streets buzzed with activity. Main Street was blocked off with saw horses and police cruisers, and venders were busy setting up tents filled with fresh produce, arts and crafts, and flea market items.

"Are you ready to go?" Darby asked hopefully.

"Home?" Willy asked in surprise.

"Yeah."

"We can't go home yet, Darby. We haven't seen the

flea market. And besides, what is that wonderful smell?"

Their noses led them to the church hall, where the Women's Auxiliary was putting on a pancake feast. Darby paid the eight-dollar charge and they walked inside. The hall had been decorated in pink and white streamers, and long buffet tables with white paper tablecloths stretched from end to end. The firemen's wives and daughters moved between the tables, refilling coffee cups and replenishing giant, strawberry-shaped bowls of fruit. Darby scanned the crowd and saw people lounging casually, speaking easily together as they ate. Mostly locals, he thought.

He guided Willy to the back window, where red-faced women filled plates with handfuls of bacon and buckwheat pancakes the size of Frisbees. As they took their seats at an empty table, he glanced at the faces around him. There were no shocked expressions, no surreptitious whispers. Just a bunch of people eating breakfast, he thought. So far so good.

~ * ~

After a delicious but heavy feast of griddlecakes and bacon, Willy and Darby wandered down Main Street, where a cornucopia of festival tents had sprung up. There were craft booths featuring homemade candles and quilts, whimsical Cheshire cats and checkerboards carved out of wood. There were tents of fresh fruits and vegetables, and tables filled with jewelry. Willy stopped to admire a bracelet, a delicate braided chain with a turquoise stone set in the center, and Darby bought it for her. Despite the headache that was threatening, Willy couldn't remember when she'd spent a more enjoyable day. She loved the festive atmosphere, the cheerful chatter, the uncomplicated, down-home charm that only a small town could provide. Darby waited patiently as she perused every tent, but Willy sensed he was ill at ease, out of his element, as if he would rather be anywhere but there.

"Thanks for being patient with me, Darby," she said. "Just one more booth, okay?"

"Take your time, Willy," he said, but there was no mistaking the weary tone in his voice. Not wanting to take advantage of his patience, she passed by the next three booths, until a tent filled with antiques beckoned. Inside, she was greeted by the unmistakable scent of days gone by. She dropped to her knees beside a crate of old books, sorted through it, and found a near pristine copy of *Gone with the Wind.* Hugging it to her, she moved on to a display of old hats. There were glass jars filled with marbles, old cigar boxes, and other things she couldn't begin to identify. Darby's mood had lightened, and he seemed to enjoy the antiques booth as much as she did. He possessed an amazing amount of knowledge about old things and appeared to enjoy filling her in on the items and their former uses.

She came across a small, wire cage on a long wooden handle.

"What do you suppose this was used for?"

"That's a soap saver," he said.

She turned the object over in her hand. "How does it work?"

"Back in the Depression years people didn't have the luxury of wasting anything. Not even a bar of soap." He opened the metal clasp on top of the cage. "They used to collect the slivers and put them in this basket." Closing the clasp, he added, "Then they would swirl this around in their wash water, and maybe have enough soap left for a bath or two."

"Amazing." Willy held onto the soap saver, deciding it would look nice in her kitchen. "How do you know all of this?"

He shrugged. "I read a lot."

As they were leaving the tent, Willy noticed an old washbowl and pitcher set. It was pretty and delicate, white porcelain with a ring of tiny gold leaves and butterflies embossed around its center. The price was more than she wanted to pay, but she could not get herself to pass it up. "I'm going to buy this."

"A washbowl and pitcher? Your cottage does have a shower, you know."

"It's called impulse buying, Darby. Women are famous for it." She paid for the items and they left the tent.

"Okay, boss, now what?"

"Lunch. And then home."

They walked to the village square, where the food tents were located. The scent of grilled sausage hung tantalizingly in the air, drawing them in. A large sandwich board outside the tent advertised hot dogs, Italian sausage, and French fries. Willy stopped to study the board, and didn't notice the woman approaching until she was feet away.

"How's them flowers working out for ya?"

She turned, startled, and found herself looking at the farmer's wife. "Oh, fine."

"How are you liking Baker's Gully?"

"I like it very well," she said.

The woman grinned. "Glad to hear it. If you're ever in the market for fresh strawberries or peaches this summer, you know where to find 'em. Best prices in town."

Willy smiled at her brazenness. "I'll certainly keep that in mind."

The woman lingered, her eyes sweeping over Darby with curiosity before wandering back to Willy. "So have they started surveying for the park yet?"

To Willy's surprise, Darby spoke up. "What park?"

~ * ~

"You must not be from around here."

Darby held her gaze, clearly not in the mood for her information seeking, and firmly repeated the question.

"What park?"

"It's been all over the newspapers," she told him. "Seems the state is putting in a park up on Baker's Gully. Supposed to cover two hundred some odd acres. They're going to put in hiking trails, picnic areas, even a swimming pool."

As the farmer's wife continued to spout information about the park, Willy saw a stricken expression come over Darby's face. He looked troubled, she thought, and suddenly tired, as if the day had taken a toll on him. She looked at him closely, wondering how it was that she had never noticed the strands of silver at his temples, the tiny lines around his eyes.

"Are you all right, Darby?" she asked, as the woman strode away.

"Sure," he said unconvincingly.

"Are you upset about the park?"

"Nah," he said, but she could plainly see he was. She sensed his urgency to leave, and felt selfish for having kept him for so long.

"Darby, I'm starting to get a headache. Do you mind if we skip lunch?"

~ * ~

Darby loaded Willy's purchases into the back of the truck and slid into the driver's seat, forcing himself to act naturally, to stay calm. Inside, he was sick with dread, his mind racing in a hundred directions. He'd known his twenty acres in Baker's Gully would not provide him sanctuary forever. Of course he'd known that. The winds of change were blowing, had been blowing for quite some time. He'd known that someday, it would all come to an end. He cast a sideways glance at Willy. She smiled at him, and he felt his heart shatter. He'd let himself believe in a fairy tale, a happy story that didn't have a ghost of a chance of coming true.

"Thanks, Darby," she said.

"For what?"

"For today. It was lovely."

"My pleasure, darlin'."

He turned the key in the ignition. The truck sputtered and coughed. Willy eyed him with surprise. "Uh-oh. That doesn't sound good."

With a sinking heart, Darby popped the hood and got out of the truck. The battery cables, sparkling clean just hours before, were encrusted with corrosion. He retrieved a screwdriver from the truck and scraped them clean, then wiped them off with a hankie as best he could and returned to the driver's seat. He lifted his eyes to the cloudless sky and screamed a silent, one-word prayer. *Please.*

He turned the key. The engine fired and he slowly let out his breath. Driving home, he was grateful that Willy didn't seem to want to talk. He was too distracted to keep up his end of a conversation. He felt tired and unfocused, depleted. *Old.*

Back at the cottage, he carried the washbowl and pitcher into the kitchen. Willy had gone ahead to unlock the door, and upon entering, he saw her remove a prescription bottle from the cupboard and unscrew the cap. She shook three pills into her palm and swallowed them dry. "Headache?" he asked.

"Too much sun, I think."

"A bad one?"

"No." She tried to smile, but he could see that the day in town had taken its toll on her, as well. "Maybe I'll go in and lie down for awhile."

"I could use a siesta myself," he said, and kissed her lightly on the cheek.

"See you this evening?" she asked.

"You bet."

~ * ~

Back home, Darby studied his face in the mirror. He noted the faint laugh lines around his eyes, the strands of silver in his hair. It was happening quickly.

His body was betraying him.

The words the farmer's wife had spoken echoed in his head.

...some two hundred odd acres... hiking trails... picnic areas... even going to put in a swimming pool. A sweat broke out on his forehead.

He thought of an old woman, and a silver charm buried deep in the earth.

Then he thought of Willy, and he prayed to God there was enough magic left to save her.

Thirteen

After Darby left, Willy stretched out on her bed, fully clothed, and crashed into a deep, dreamless sleep. She awoke hours later in a pitch-black room. Disoriented, she groped for the clock on her nightstand. *Four a.m. Good Lord.*

She'd only meant to take a short nap, to ease her pounding head, and instead ended up sleeping for thirteen hours. She crawled out of bed and padded through the still, dark rooms and into the kitchen.

"Might as well get the day started," she murmured.

She measured out four scoops of coffee, added a carafe of water, and set the coffee maker to perking. By the time her coffee was ready, she felt wide awake and completely refreshed. She couldn't remember when she'd slept more soundly. It was as if the valley had cast some sort of spell over her. *Like Sleeping Beauty,* she thought with a wry smile, except that she hadn't awakened to a breathless kiss. Her thoughts bridged to Darby and she wondered whether he had come back last night. Had he discovered her sleeping and gone away, not wanting to disturb her? Or maybe he had slept just as soundly.

She wandered to the window and looked out at the darkness. She thought back over their day at the festival and how it seemed to deplete him. He hadn't wanted to go in the first place and it was good of him to take her. The thought sparked an idea and she moved to the cupboards and took inventory. Flour. Sugar. Shortening. She'd stop by The Farmer's Wife as soon as it opened, she decided. She'd buy a bag of apples and bake him the pie he'd asked for. She poured a cup of coffee and carried it to the porch, wondering how she would fill the four hours between now and then.

As she sipped her coffee, her thoughts returned to the festival and the interesting things she'd bought. She went back inside, brought them out, and spread them across the table. She tried on the bracelet Darby bought her, admiring its intricate detailing. She flipped through the pages of *Gone with the Wind* and opened and closed the clasp on the soap saver. Finally she pulled the washbowl and pitcher from their box and carefully unwrapped the tissue paper the merchant had wrapped them in. She ran her fingers over the smooth porcelain and the delicate gold detailing. She carried the set inside and contemplated every corner of the house, trying to decide on the best place to display her new treasure, and finally decided on a corner in the alcove off the living room.

She moved the small round table away from the rocking chair, set the bowl and pitcher on it, and stood back to study the effect. No, that wasn't quite right. The bowl overhung the edge of the table by two inches, making the display look awkward and off balance. What she needed was an old-fashioned teacart, or some sort of cabinet. Maybe she would go back to the festival today, have another look around the antiques tent. The thought exhausted her and she quickly discarded it.

Feeling hungry, she toasted a bagel, topped off her coffee cup, and returned to the porch. She glanced at the battered table and smiled. Of course.

When she and Sid had gone up to the attic to store

some of Willy's things, they'd noticed the table and benches in a dusty corner. They'd finagled them down the steep attic steps and out to the porch, nearly breaking their backs in the process. Thinking back, it seemed to Willy that there had been more furniture up there. She and Sid hadn't bothered to investigate the attic further, but it was certainly worth a look.

When she'd finished her bagel, she dug a flashlight out of the broom closet and climbed the attic stairs. A yank on the tattered string suspended from the ceiling yielded only a shallow pool of light and she was glad she'd thought to bring the flashlight. She switched it on and walked toward the back of the attic. The air was humid, heavy, despite the coolness of the morning. The hair on the nape of her neck prickled and she hesitated. It was almost as though she wasn't alone, as though a sad, brooding presence hung in the air around her. She took a cautious step, telling herself she was being silly.

A shot rang out, shattering the quiet, and she screamed. She stood still for a moment, her heart pounding, listening. She heard the sound again and realized it was nothing more than a tree branch smacking against the tin roof. Pushing out a breath, she continued on.

She crept to the back corner where several pieces of furniture were draped in bed sheets. Pulling back the coverings, she discovered a double dresser, a small chest of drawers, an easel, and two easy chairs. Nothing she could use, she realized with disappointment. She trained the flashlight beam on the boxes that were queued against the wall. There were four of them, good-sized, but not large enough to hold furniture. She squinted at the bold, black print on the sides. *Marilyn.*

She stared at the boxes with curiosity, wondering what was in them. She knew she shouldn't snoop; any way you looked at it, it was wrong to go through someone's things... But obviously there was nothing in them anyone cared about. She ran her hand over the closest box and wiped the dust on her pants. The boxes had obviously been sitting here a while. Maybe even years.

Her curiosity finally got the best of her and she sank to her knees beside the box. Old and brittle, the packing tape peeled away easily. Swallowing the last of her guilt, she opened the flaps and peered inside.

Marilyn was obviously an artist. The box contained a myriad of art supplies; blank canvases, brushes, half-used tubes of paint. Feeling mildly disappointed, Willy set it aside and tore into the second box.

This one was full of clothes. She pulled the items out, one by one, and studied them. Judging from the sizes of the garments, Marilyn had been blessed with an ample chest and a tiny waist. She also had expensive tastes. The clothes were stylish and expensively made, even if they were two decades out of date. She considered the neon colors and the wide, padded shoulders. Everything in the box screamed *'eighties!*

She moved on to the third box, not a trace of guilt remaining. This one contained a mix-matched variety of items: dishes, silverware, books, a pair of brass candlesticks.

The fourth box was the largest, and Willy had purposely saved it for last. She peeled off the tape and pulled back the thin layer of tissue paper, expecting to find more art supplies. Her breath caught as she pulled out the canvas. It was a watercolor painting of the riverbank in autumn. It was eerily lifelike, the sort of painting a person could get lost in. Staring at the elaborate details, she could almost hear the chortling of the river, the volley of birdsong in the air. The water was clear and blue, and all around it, trees exploded in color. The artist's keen eye had missed nothing. She'd even captured a doe hiding in the reeds. Willy ran her hand reverently over the signature in the corner. Marilyn Carpenter. The painting would look magnificent hanging above the fireplace. In any case, it was too pretty to be tucked away in a box. She set it aside, making a mental note to ask Darby's permission to hang it, and eagerly reached for the next canvas.

This one was a still life of the cottage. It looked much the same as now, except the roses had been trimmed back, exposing the front door. Beneath that canvas was one other, a half-completed painting of the river in winter. Marilyn had obviously spent some time in Baker's Gully, had seen all of the seasons come and go, and committed their beauty to canvas. The winter scene was most striking of all. Why hadn't she finished it?

At the bottom of the box Willy discovered a sketchpad, and she eagerly flipped it open. The first few pages contained generic nature sketches: trees, a brown rabbit, a cluster of forget-me-nots. They were amazingly lifelike, and with each new page Willy's admiration for Marilyn Carpenter grew. There were a few sketches of the cottage, and, Willy noted with surprise, one of Darby's cabin.

She flipped through the pages until she came to a sketch that stopped her cold. It was a sketch of Darby, leaning casually against his truck. She shined the flashlight on the picture, amazed at Marilyn's talent, and how perfectly she had captured Darby's essence. It was obvious she'd known him well.

The last sketch in the book was one of Darby and Lucky playing in a meadow, much as they had the day he'd taken Willy to hunt for long berries. She traced her finger over the image of the dog, almost able to feel his fur, and the silver dollar-sized bald patch beneath his collar. As she closed the sketchbook and tucked it back into the box, she noticed a large manila envelope. It was sealed, but having come this far, she couldn't see any harm in opening it.

She pulled out a handful of black and white photos:

the river, a brown rabbit, Darby's cabin. She went through the thin stack, viewing a photo of Darby leaning against his truck, one of him and Lucky splashing in the river. There was a photo of a woman with dark hair and beautiful dark eyes.

"Marilyn," Willy whispered.

The last photo was one of Darby and Marilyn together. They stood, arms around one another, smiling. On impulse Willy turned the photo over. She stared in disbelief at the words that were written in cursive across the back. *Darby and Marilyn, 1986.*

She turned the photo over, stared at it. "How can that be?" she murmured.

Darby couldn't be more than thirty years old, and yet, this photo was dated twenty years in the past. He would have been approximately ten when the photo was taken, but here he was, looking just the same as today.

She shuffled through the pictures again, looking for an explanation. Her rational mind told her that the photo was of Darby's parents. He'd plainly told her he was Darby Sullivan the Third. A lot of children resembled their fathers, except...

How did Lucky get sealed up in a twenty-year-old envelope with Darby's parents?

Of course, it could be another dog...

A chocolate lab with the exact same markings, a small voice fretted, *and the same exact bald spot beneath his collar?*

She scoured her memory for what little information Darby had shared with her.

Thrown away...

I had three meals a day, and a roof over my head. And that dog...

Judging from the clothes in the box, Marilyn had been anything but poor. And if Darby Senior and Marilyn had continued to live here at the cottage, then why send their child away?

Darby's words echoed in her head.

I was raised on a farm. A place for kids who had nowhere else to be...

Something broke free inside her, a memory that had eluded her that night.

It was her first day of kindergarten. She was five years old, afraid of the austere, brick building, afraid of being left alone. Crying, she held tightly to Eva's hand.

"Let go now, child. Let go!"

"Grandma, I don't want to go."

Eva smacked her upside the head. *"It's only for a day, Willow. You keep this up and I'll send you off to the poor farm."*

She dried her tears on the hem of her dress and looked at her grandmother, wide-eyed. "*What's the poor farm, Grandma?"*

"Lucky for you they don't have them any more," Eva said, straightening Willy's rummage sale dress. "But it was a place where poor people sent their children to live, during the Great Depression. Kids didn't go to school, in those days. They dug ditches and picked rocks..."

The Great Depression...

"Back in the Depression years people didn't have the luxury of wasting things. Not even a bar of soap."

A hundred thoughts clamored for Willy's attention, but none of them made sense. There had to be a logical explanation, but she couldn't begin to guess what it was.

She stumbled back down the stairs, still carrying the photos. She moved mechanically, pouring another cup of coffee, trying to think. She sat at the table staring at the photos until six-thirty, then went to the phone and dialed Sid's number.

Sid answered groggily on the third ring.

"Hello, Sid?" she choked out.

"Willy?" Sid's voice was alarmed, instantly alert. "What's wrong?"

"Nothing, I hope. Did I wake you?"

"I had to get up in ten minutes anyway. And I'd rather wake up to the sound of your voice than my obnoxious alarm clock. So what's up?"

"Would you do something for me, Sid?"

"Name it."

"Would you get on the Internet and do a web search for Darby Sullivan, and another for an artist named Marilyn Carpenter?"

"Wait a minute." There was a pause, then the faint scratch of pencil against paper. "Okay, Darby Sullivan. What's this about, anyway?"

"Sid, the thing is... could you just do it, no questions asked?"

"All right. No problem. Anything specific you're looking for?"

"Try to link the name Darby Sullivan with Murphy's Crossing. Or a town called West Dover. Go back to 1930. See what you can come up with from then to now."

"I'll see what I can do."

"Thanks, Sid."

"You're killing me, here. Sure you can't tell me what this is about?"

Willy wanted desperately to tell Sid. But tell her what, exactly? Knowing how crazy her suspicions would sound, she said, "Not yet."

She took a hot shower, hoping it would calm her nerves, which were suddenly stretched tight. Fifteen minutes later she emerged from the bathroom, dressed in a pair of denim shorts and a tee-shirt. She checked to make sure her answering machine was on then grabbed her keys from the counter and headed out the door. It might be hours before

Sid got back to her. Meanwhile, she was going to drive out to West Dover. And hopefully she would return with some answers.

Fourteen

She wasn't home. From where he stood on the path, Darby had a full view of Willy's driveway. The Explorer wasn't in it.

The disappointment he felt was completely out of proportion. Knowing that, he swallowed it down and continued walking. Maybe she ran out of milk or coffee, and had made a quick dash to town. His thoughts brightened, then immediately clouded again, like a temperamental summer sky. Maybe she hadn't gotten her fill of the Strawberry Festival yesterday and had gone back for more. The thought made him strangely uneasy. Knowing the visit was pointless now, he forged ahead anyway. Maybe she'd left him a note.

He cursed himself for not coming back last night. He'd only planned to rest for a few hours, just long enough to replenish his depleted energy. He'd planned to invite Willy to the cabin for dinner, and maybe a moonlight swim. He'd awakened early in the evening and tried to rouse himself from bed, his longing to be with Willy battling with the exhaustion that seemed to have settled deep in his bones. His fatigue finally won out and he fell back asleep, not awakening again until mid-morning. Forgoing breakfast, he quickly showered and dressed, plucked the strands of gray from his hair, and set off down the path. And now she wasn't home.

Stepping onto the porch, his eyes were immediately drawn to the table. He assessed the coffee cup, the plate of toast crumbs, and the large yellow envelope that sat between them. *Not my business,* he told himself, but uneasiness began to swirl in his gut, and a small, worrisome voice whispered in his ear, telling him to look inside the envelope. His heart tripped irrhythmically as he pulled out the photographs and studied them. "Oh, God."

A ferocious pain stabbed his heart as he looked into Marilyn's pretty, smiling face, a pain that was quickly replaced by panic. She knew. Willy had discovered his secret, and now she'd left him. Just as Marilyn had.

Steeling himself, he tried the door. Finding it unlocked, he stepped inside the cottage. He glanced around the kitchen. Everything seemed to be exactly as it had been the day before. He made a quick pass through the living room, and into the bedroom. He threw open the closet doors and looked inside. All of Willy's clothes hung neatly on their hangers, her shoes lined up in a tidy row on the floor beneath them. A check of her dresser drawers revealed all of her underthings neatly folded, her shorts and tee-shirts still intact. He noticed a jewelry box on top of her dresser. Lifting the cover, he discovered earrings, necklaces, and the bracelet he'd bought for her the day before. He slid open a small drawer and discovered a roll of money. Even if Willy had fled in horror, leaving her clothes and jewelry behind, she certainly would have taken her cash. He let out the breath he hadn't realized he was holding. She was coming back.

He tidied his mess the best he could and stepped back out onto the porch. He slid the photos back in the envelope, not looking at them. She was coming back. He still had time.

He gazed out at the river, trying to think rationally,

logically. Yes, Willy knew more than she had the day before, but really, what did she know? That a beautiful woman and a man had loved one another twenty years ago... A man who appeared to be him? Things were not always what they appeared. That was all she really needed to know. For now.

~ * ~

It was after eight o'clock when Willy's Explorer crossed over the bridge that separated Brookdale Township from West Dover. Though not much bigger than Murphy's Crossing, the town was much, much tidier. Cruising down the five blocks that comprised Main Street, she took note of the crisp, white storefronts, the baskets of impatience and blue lobelia that were suspended from the wrought iron streetlamps. In the third block there was a fountain with a statue of Jesse Dover, the town's founding father, and a sign that proudly proclaimed: Welcome to West Dover. A friendly community within a scenic valley. Founded 1818.

She made another pass down Main Street and pulled up in front of the library, an impressive red-brick structure with spanking white trim. She parked the truck, got out, and walked up to the front door. It was locked. She looked around for a sign and saw one taped to the front window:

SUMMER HOURS:
Sunday and Monday--Closed
Tuesday through Friday--10 a.m. to 7 p.m.
Saturday--noon to 4 p.m.

"Great," she muttered. "What am I supposed to do until noon?"

She walked back to the Explorer, trying to formulate a plan. Most libraries, even in small towns, had at least one computer available to the public nowadays. The library had seemed a logical place to start. But as they said, every plan had a flaw. She'd just have to think of something else.

Her gaze wandered across the street and she noticed a diner. The hand-painted sign in the window cheerfully announced: Granny's Restaurant. Breakfast, Lunch and Dinner served. *Okay,* she thought. *Granny's looks like as good a place as any to regroup.*

The tinkle of sleigh bells announced her arrival as she walked through the front door. A handful of people occupied the tables, while two old men sat at the lunch counter up front. If they were aware of the smoking regulations the state had recently passed, they chose to ignore them. The waitress, a fifty-something woman with a bleached blonde ponytail and bright blue eye shadow, looked up from the table full of old women she'd been chatting with. She'd been refilling their coffee cups, and now her pot hovered in mid-air as she sized Willy up. Finally, she smiled.

"Anyplace you want to sit will be fine, hon. I'll be with you in a sec."

Willy slid into a booth near the back of the diner. Her glance took in the upholstered pink booths, the black and white checkered floor. A number of old photos were displayed prominently on the walls, some high school football player's long-lost glory days, she noted, along with his trophies and his faded letterman's sweater. Despite herself, she was charmed. While the city was filled with quaint cafes that spent a fortune on furnishings and claptrap to make them look old-fashioned, Willy got the impression Granny's was the real deal.

Within moments the waitress appeared at her table. She wore a frilly pink apron, the name Millie embroidered across the pocket. "Menu?" she asked hopefully.

"Umm, no. Just coffee, thanks." Noting the disappointment on Millie's face, Willy quickly amended, "And maybe a slice of that delicious looking blueberry pie up there."

"Oh, you won't be sorry." Millie beamed. "Granny

makes all of her pies fresh every morning."

"There really is a Granny?" Willy asked in surprise.

"Of course." Millie filled her coffee cup and bustled away, returning moments later with a thick slab of pie. "I take it you're not from around these parts."

"The city, actually."

"Really?" Millie studied her as if she were a fascinating insect she'd just caught. "What brings you to West Dover?"

Willy considered her answer carefully. Maybe Millie could help. "I'm looking for a farm."

Millie's smile broadened. "Are you, now? Well then, you've come to the right place. These hills are full of them." She waved her hand toward the window with a flourish. "We're the biggest potato-producing town in the state! You looking for work?"

Willy hid a smile. "Actually, I'm looking for a particular farm. One run by the county. A home for abandoned children."

Millie's brows knit in thought. "A farm run by the county?"

"Yes. Would you know where that is?"

"A farm for abandoned..." Willy saw a light bulb go off in Millie's head. "You don't mean Brookhaven?"

"Yes, that's exactly what I mean," Willy said, not missing a beat.

"Mercy, child. They closed Brookhaven down more than forty years ago!"

Willy felt her stomach lurch, and feared she'd be sick. Forcing a smile, she said, "I realize that, Millie. I simply wondered whether it would be possible to see the property as it is today. You see, my grandfather grew up at Brookhaven. I'm researching my family tree, and I was hoping... Well, I don't really know what I was hoping for."

"Tell you the truth, I'm not really sure where it is."

Millie's face became a mask of concern, as if Willy's dilemma were of utmost importance. "Sit tight, honey, while I go and ask Granny. There's not a piece of property in this town that ol' gal doesn't know like the back of her hand."

She bustled away again, and Willy found herself alone, with yet another puzzle piece that didn't fit. The farm had closed down forty years ago, and yet she was certain Darby had specified a county-run farm in West Dover. Was she losing her mind?

Millie returned to the table, followed by an old woman. "This is her, Granny," Millie said.

The old woman regarded Willy through a pair of wire-rimmed bifocals, then said, "Name's Peg O'Dell. Most people around here just call me Granny. Mind if I sit?" Not waiting for an answer, she eased herself into the booth across from Willy. "Now, Millie here tells me you're wanting to see the old county farm?"

"That's what she says," Millie interjected. "Says her grandfather grew up there."

"That'll do, Millie." Granny gave the waitress a pointed glance, and Millie reluctantly went back to filling coffee cups. Granny fixed her gaze on Willy. "What was your grandfather's name, child?"

His name? Good Lord... Willy smiled politely. "Sullivan. His name was Rory Sullivan."

"Rory Sullivan..." The old woman drew the name out, as if testing the sound of it on her tongue.

"But my family's not originally from here," Willy hastily added. "They immigrated here in the late 'twenties. From Ireland. When the Depression hit, well, they couldn't afford to feed Rory, so they turned him over to the county."

Granny smiled sadly. "Those were tough times, child. You can't blame the lad's parents."

"Oh, I know. I was just hoping for a look at the place. Can you tell me where it is?"

"Certainly I can tell you," she said. "But I'm afraid it's not going to help you. You won't find much of anything there except planks and two-by-fours. It's a lumberyard now. Has been for twenty years."

"I see," Willy said, unable to mask her disappointment.

"Tell you what you could do, you could pop over to the Historical Society. They surely have photographs. And probably some documents, too. It's a big white building, about two blocks down."

It was a new starting point and Willy was grateful to the old woman for suggesting it. She paid for her pie and stepped back out into the sunshine, feeling oddly chilled. Either the tumor had begun to damage her brain, making her remember things that had never been said, or Darby was hiding something from her. Any way you looked at it she came out on the losing end.

The West Dover Historical Society was located in a former blacksmith's shop and looked as though it had been renovated just enough to satisfy the local Code Enforcement Officer. The wide plank floors were unvarnished, as were the two-hundred-year-old barn boards that made up the interior walls. Stepping inside, Willy was immediately aware of a rise in temperature. An oscillating fan stood in the corner, doing little more than shifting the scents of old paper and warm, trapped air.

"Good morning."

Startled, Willy glanced behind the glass display counter, where a bookish looking man of about sixty watched her expectantly, as if he'd been waiting for her. "You must be the young lady Granny sent over, the young lady looking for information about Brookhaven?"

Willy was surprised and didn't bother to hide it. "News travels fast."

A blush crept up his neck and spread across his face.

"Forgive us. We don't have much else to talk about, 'round here."

I guess not, Willy thought.

"I've started pulling documents for you. Come." She followed him to a small, airless room in the back of the building, where six mismatched chairs sat around a large, polished table. "I thought you might like to look them over in privacy," the man said, indicating a pair of folders in the center of the table.

"Thank you very much." Willy sat down and reached for the folder on top, her heart pounding in anticipation. She felt lightheaded, dizzy, but maybe it was just the heat.

The man returned with a file drawer full of neatly catalogued photos and set them down beside the folders. "This is all we have. I'm afraid you won't find specific names of the children who lived at Brookhaven. That information is classified."

"I'm sure I'll find something of use," Willy said. "Thank you so much. You've been very helpful."

"If you wouldn't mind signing the register, it gives us a record of who's visited." He handed her a clipboard. She signed the form on the top and handed it back to him. He hovered in the doorway for a moment, like a proud and nervous parent, then finally he left her alone. Taking a breath to fortify herself, Willy opened the first folder.

She read of the founding of the village in 1818, its prosperity with the coming of the railroad, its staggering growth as immigrant families poured into town, seeking employment. She read of its crash into poverty, along with the rest of the nation, in the Great Depression of the 1930s, and the opening of Brookhaven.

Brookhaven was originally a family-run farm owned by a couple named Tom and Mary Deuel. With more compassion than money, the Deuels began to take in some of the swelling numbers of unwanted children. Two years and eighteen children later, near bankruptcy, they petitioned the county for help. The county responded with an offer to assume the mortgage payments on the farm. They would oversee the operation and designate Tom and Mary Deuel as caretakers of the facility for as long as they lived.

Willy waded through the documents, feeling increasingly dizzy. She massaged the base of her neck, where a dull throbbing promised to bloom into a migraine. She read of the facility's evolution from its humble beginnings in the 'thirties, through the stiff-upper-lip war years of the 'forties, when Brookhaven had boasted the largest Victory Garden in the county, and up to its eventual closing with the implementation of the county's foster care system in 1959.

~ * ~

She closed the last folder, feeling frustrated. She knew little more now than when she sat down at the table two hours ago. The headache had progressed from a dull ache to sharp, stabbing pains. She considered calling it a day, but stubbornly reconsidered. Having come this far she might as well see it through to the end. With a sigh, she reached for the box of pictures.

They started in 1959 and worked backward. She flipped through photos of the house and barns, of children working in the fields. After those, there were photos of a schoolroom, a kitchen with a brick fireplace, and several large, dormitory-style bedrooms with bunk beds lining the walls.

She worked back through the 'forties: grainy photos of children celebrating birthdays, carving pumpkins. After an hour she pushed the box away, not sure whether she could continue. Her head was raging, and the photos, blurring before her eyes.

"How are you doing back here?" The old man

appeared in the doorway and she gave him a weary smile.

"Fine."

"Would you like a glass of water?" he asked, his concern showing plainly on his face.

"That would be wonderful."

He returned with the water, set it down beside her, and retreated. Willy reached into her purse, shook two painkillers from her prescription bottle, and swallowed them. She massaged her cat-scratched eyes for a moment before returning to the box of pictures.

She had progressed to the late 1930s. *Not more than a couple dozen photos left,* she reassured herself.

1939... Tom and Mary Deuel, children splashing in a creek, children with their heads bowed, saying grace over a Thanksgiving turkey.

1938... A photo of the living room, a Christmas tree set up in the corner. Several children were posed in front of the tree. A boy of around ten held a small, brown puppy. A Labrador retriever. Willy started at the photo, suddenly chilled.

They brought him to the farm when he was a pup. He was a Christmas gift for all of us, but he seemed to love me the most. Maybe he knew I needed him the most.

She expelled a breath, forced her eyes closed, opened them again, willing them to focus. She told herself she was being ridiculous. The photo was nearly seventy years old, grainy and out of focus. She stared at the puppy, then at the dark-haired boy. It could have been any dog, any boy, and yet... There was something, some familiar haunted look about his eyes. Willy clamped her hand over her mouth, fearing she'd be sick. She shot a hurried glance through the doorway before shoving the photo into her purse. She stood on shaking legs and returned to the front room.

"Did you get through it all?" the old man asked politely.

Not yet, Willy thought. *And maybe not ever.*

She thanked him for letting her peruse the documents and fled the building. She stumbled back to her Explorer, opened her purse, and dug for her keys. The boy in the photo stared back at her. She quickly zipped up her purse, unable to think about him any more today, unable to reconcile the thoughts that were taking shape in her tortured brain. The thoughts that offered an unbelievable solution to the puzzle. The corner piece, unbelievable, and yet, the only one that fit. The piece that said Darby Sullivan had been reincarnated.

Fifteen

It was the middle of the afternoon when Darby's footsteps once again turned down the path. *Surely she'll be home by now,* he thought. When the cottage came into view, he squinted at the driveway. Still empty. The uneasiness he'd felt all morning evolved into full-fledged fear. *Where could she have gone?*

Contemplating the possibilities, he walked to the end of the path, scanning the road for as far as he could see. There was no sign of her. He was considering whether or not he should go and look for her when a black sedan rolled into view. It cruised past slowly, then made a three-point turn and came back. The driver's side window slid down to reveal a man in a crisp, white shirt and black slacks. Darby folded his arms across his chest and waited for the man to state his business.

"Excuse me," the man said. "Can you tell me where I can find a man by the name of Darby Sullivan?"

Darby gave him a cold stare. "That would be me."

A shadow of doubt crossed the man's face. "Is there more than one? The Darby Sullivan I'm looking for would be an older gentleman."

"What's this about?"

"Carl Davis. State Parks Commission." He flashed a

set of credentials. "I need to speak to Mr. Sullivan on an urgent matter."

"I'm the only Darby Sullivan around here."

The man's glance scanned the cottage before returning to Darby's face. "This your property?"

"Yep."

"Nice place."

Darby continued to stare at him in stony silence and Davis shifted uncomfortably in his seat. "I can see you're not a man who likes to waste time, Mr. Sullivan, so I'll cut right to the chase. I'm going to assume you already know why I'm here."

"No idea," Darby lied.

"You signed for a certified letter last week. Didn't you read it?"

Darby held his gaze. "I must have misplaced it."

"The gist of it, Mr. Sullivan, is that you are in a position to make a lot of money."

"Not interested."

"Mr. Sullivan, this land of yours is prime property, and my department is willing to pay top dollar for it. The state wants to set it aside, preserve it, *protect* it. That's not such a bad thing, now is it?"

"Protect it?" Darby glared at him, incredulous. "By putting in hot dogs grills and a swimming pool?"

"So you did read the letter."

"Let me save you some time, Davis, and a whole lot of aggravation. This land is not for sale. Not now. Not ever."

Carl Davis' eyes narrowed to slits as his tone took on the texture of chipped ice. "Well now, it doesn't seem to me that that's your decision to make." He pulled a clipboard from between the seats and flipped through his paperwork. "According to our records, this land belongs to an old man. Now, unless you've got one hell of a plastic surgeon, you're about fifty years too young to be the Darby Sullivan we're looking for."

Darby began to experience a sinking, drowning sensation. "He's my grandfather."

"And you're his legal power of attorney?"

Darby said nothing.

"Fact is, I shouldn't even be talking to you about this," Davis said smugly. "Where can I find the old man?"

"You can't."

"Then against my better judgment I'm going to have to let you act as go-between." He held out a thick, business-sized envelope. "Give these to your grandfather to look over. Tell him it's the best deal he's going to get, so I suggest he take it and run. And see that it doesn't get *misplaced.*"

Darby stared at the envelope, making no move to take it. "Or what?"

"Or you'll both come out of the deal empty-handed." A malicious smile crossed his face. He had Darby by the balls and they both knew it. "The old man has thirty days to respond to our generous *offer.* If we don't hear from him by then, we'll take his silence as consent. Have a nice day." He threw the packet on the road at Darby's feet and drove away.

As he watched the sedan disappear around the bend, Darby once again got the sensation of the ground falling away. It was all unraveling, coming apart. He felt like a drowning man in an ocean, not a lifeboat in sight, not a damn thing he could do to save himself.

~ * ~

Willy turned the Explorer into the driveway and turned off the engine. If she had ever been more glad to see the cottage, she couldn't remember it. She sat behind the wheel for a long moment, trembling, trying to reassure herself.

The last five hours had been sheer hell.

When she left the town of West Dover it was nearly noon. Her head was pounding and her insides felt like they were on fire. She knew better than to take her pain medication on an empty stomach, and couldn't think why she hadn't waited. Thinking a cold drink and a sandwich might help, she followed the signs to a roadside diner. The tuna sandwich she'd eaten had helped calm her stomach, but by then she was seeing double. Leaving town, a succession of wrong turns took her miles out of her way. It hadn't helped she had to keep pulling over as wave after wave of dizziness engulfed her. All of her crying hadn't helped matters. Her eyes were puffed and swollen now, and her head, near exploding. She'd never known such agony.

For the first time since her diagnosis Willy wanted to die. She eased her head back against the headrest and closed her eyes, willing death to find her, longing for the eternal rest she'd so often heard about.

What could have been moments or hours later, she heard a soft tap against her window. She kept her eyes closed, ignoring it. The door opened, and he softly said her name. She opened her eyes, and the expression on Darby's face went from one of concern to one of absolute alarm.

"Willy, what is it? What's wrong?"

"I can't..." She tried to speak, but managed only a whimper. "I can't talk to you right now, Darby. I'm sorry."

"Your head." It wasn't a question.

She nodded. Despite her resolve, fresh tears sprouted. "Oh, God, Darby, it hurts. It hurts so bad."

She didn't resist as his arms went around her, as he unfastened her seatbelt and gently lifted her from the truck. She crumbled against him, her arms clasped tightly around his waist, as if she might draw upon his strength.

"Darby, I feel like I'm dying."

"Shhh." His arms, rock-solid around her, stood in sharp contrast to the gentleness in his voice. "It'll be all right."

She choked on a sob.

"I know, darlin'." One hand gently massaged her neck, her head, while the other held her fast. "Just breathe. We'll get through it."

She laid her head against his chest as he rocked her, ever so gently, back and forth. His past and all of the questions she'd meant to ask him seemed irrelevant, now that she was with him. He held her until the sky clouded over and sprinkled them with fat drops of rain, and mercifully, mercifully, the pain began to ease.

"Better?" he asked.

"I think," she whispered.

"Good."

She looked into his eyes, and there was no mistaking the love she saw there. Not passionate love, but the kind she supposed was in a mother's eyes when she gazed upon her child.

"How do you do that?" she asked.

"Do what?"

"Take away the pain like that." Her eyes widened as a thought occurred. "Are you an angel?"

He laughed softly. "Not even close, darlin'."

The rain was falling harder but neither seemed to care. Willy snuggled back into his embrace, basking in his strength, his goodness... his love. Almost imperceptibly, she felt him tense.

"Willy, there's something I have to tell--"

No! her inner voice screamed. She was only all right when she was here, with him. And if it was all a dream, a figment of her cancer-riddled brain, she couldn't bear to know. Not today.

She pulled his head down to hers and kissed him; a lingering kiss that sent waves of desire coursing through her body. Her body and his. She could feel him responding, wanting her.

He ended the kiss abruptly. He pulled away from

her, took her by the shoulders and shook her. "Willy! There are things about me. Things you need to--"

She reached up and covered his mouth with her trembling fingers. "Do you love me, Darby?" She saw the anger drain from his eyes as all the fight went out of him.

"With all my heart."

"That's all I need to know."

She kissed him again, softly, and this time, he didn't push her away. As their kisses grew deeper, more intimate, she felt his longing, and didn't try to stop it. She wanted him, wanted all of the strength and the magic and the mystery of him. There had never been anything she wanted more. She was swept away, lovesick, whispering it over and over again. *I love you.*

A relentless rain continued to fall, washing away the last trace of doubt, as he lifted her and carried her inside.

Sixteen

It was strange waking up beside a man who wasn't Tom.

After lovemaking, Tom always preferred to keep his distance in bed. Darby's love was like nothing she ever experienced and her body responded to him in ways she never thought it capable of. Afterwards and all through the night, she lay wrapped in his loving embrace. She would have imagined the first morning with a new lover to be awkward; she was surprised at how completely comfortable she felt.

She lay with her eyes closed, taking pleasure in the feel of Darby's lean, muscular body next to hers, and the soft sound of his breathing. Soon she would have to face whatever secrets the daylight revealed, but not yet. She clung to the last remnants of night, to the memory of the love and the closeness they'd shared beneath the gentle cloak of darkness.

She felt him stir and opened her eyes to find him watching her; studying her, as though not completely convinced she was real. She smiled and lightly kissed his mouth.

"Good morning."

"Good morning."

She snuggled against him, burying her face in his chest.

"I should go home and get cleaned up," he said.

She wrapped her arms more tightly around him. "Can't you stay for just a little while longer?"

He untangled himself from her embrace, sat on the edge of the bed, and reached for his clothes. "Willy, you and I really need to talk. There's something I have to show you."

His tone was grave and Willy felt her joy evaporate as she thought of the things she discovered in West Dover. His confession was going to be monumental, terrifying, but fortified by last night's lovemaking, she felt strong enough to face it.

"Hurry back," she said. "I'll have the coffee ready."

When she heard the door close behind him, she crawled out of bed, padded to the kitchen, and started a pot of coffee. She took a quick shower and was wrapping her robe around her still-damp body when the phone rang. Pulling the robe closer around her, she hurried to the living room to answer it.

"Hello?"

"Thank God! I was getting ready to drive out there."

"Morning, Sid."

"I called you a hundred times yesterday. Didn't you get my messages?"

Glancing at the answering machine, Willy noticed the red message light's relentless flashing. "I'm sorry, Sid. I wasn't feeling well last night. I went to bed early."

"That's what I was afraid of. I don't know why you won't come and live with me, Willy. I would rest so much easier knowing you were okay."

"Sid, I'm fine. It was just a touch of the flu. So... what did you find out?"

"Nothing on Marilyn Carpenter, but I did find your guy."

Willy unconsciously gripped the arm of her chair.

"Turns out Darby Sullivan was a war hero."

"Desert Storm?"

"World War Two. He earned all kinds of medals for honor and bravery. I've got quite a few pages here. Do you want me to put them in the mail?"

"Hang onto them, Sid. I'll pick them up the next time I'm in the city."

"Care to tell me what it's about?"

"Nothing too exciting. My neighbor, Darby Sullivan the Third, is tracing his family history."

"*That's* the big mystery?"

"That's it."

"So... " She could almost feel Sid smiling. "I take it you found a way to get in his good graces."

"Ummm." Willy smiled, thinking of last night's lovemaking. "I think so."

They talked a few more minutes before hanging up. Willy leaned her head back against the chair and closed her eyes, her brain working on this new piece of the puzzle.

Back when I was in the army I'd already put in half a day by five o'clock.

I didn't know you were in the army.

It was a long time ago.

She sighed, not afraid any more, but deeply troubled. His confession was going to shake her to her foundation. "We'll get through it, Darby," she whispered. "One way or another."

~ * ~

Darby returned within the hour, freshly showered, clean-shaven, and carrying a bundle of paperwork. Willy poured them each a cup of coffee and carried them to the porch. Darby sat down on the bench across from her, a tortured expression on his face. Willy took a swallow of coffee, trying not to appear anxious as Darby composed his thoughts.

"I received a visit from the Parks Commission yesterday," he finally said.

It wasn't what she expected him to say, and the statement caught her off guard. "Oh?"

"Remember at the festival, when the woman from the farmer's market was telling us about the state wanting to open a park?"

"Yes."

"Seems my property is sitting square in the middle of their plans. They've made me an offer." He slid a sheaf of documents across the table. Willy glanced through it, then back into Darby's face.

"Are you going to sell it to them?"

"I can't." His voice cracked and he buried his face in his hands. "Oh, God. This is difficult."

Feeling his distress, Willy's gaze went back to the document. "There's a line here that says I *do not* agree to these terms. If you sign on that line it might buy you some time. We'll get a lawyer."

He drew a deep breath, released it. "Either way the signature will have to be notarized and signed by my grandfather. That's not possible, Willy."

"We'll take the documents to him, pay a notary to accompany us. We'll explain things to him, make him see..." With a look in Darby's eyes her voice trailed away.

"You don't understand."

All at once Willy realized the magnitude of the situation. "There is no grandfather," she said softly. "Is there?"

Darby shook his head.

Willy's hand crept across the table, covering his. "Darby, I understand more than you think I do. I found things... pictures and documents that lead me to believe..." She took a deep breath and forced the words out. "That

159

you've been reincarnated."

The word hung in the air between them, heavy and oppressive. Darby gazed into her eyes. He didn't look angry, as she'd feared, at the invasion of his privacy. He looked defeated. "Is that what you think?"

She nodded.

He sighed. "I didn't die and come back, Willy. The fact is... I never left." He pulled out another document and placed it before her. "I'm eighty years old." He gestured toward Lucky, who hesitantly flipped his tail. "And he's damned near seventy."

Willy stared in disbelief at the document before her. Old and yellowed, it bore Darby's name, and his date of birth: June 18, 1926.

"How is that possible?" she whispered.

Tears gathered in his eyes. "I don't know how to explain it to you... where to begin..."

She gave his hand a gentle squeeze and waited patiently while he searched for the right words. Finally, he drew a shaky breath and began.

"I was born in a little town called Brookdale. My parents were just kids themselves, unskilled and uneducated. I guess they thought they could live on love but they were wrong. When I was eight years old, the Depression hit and love wasn't enough any more. They dropped me off at a farm called Brookhaven and went to Chicago to try and find work in the factories. I never saw them again."

"Oh, Darby." She gently stroked the top of his hand.

"They did what they had to do. The only thing they could do. Brookhaven wasn't a bad sort of place. They taught us the value of hard work, and kept a roof over our heads. But it wasn't like having a real home, a real family. When they brought Lucky to the farm, it was like... well, like I finally had someone to belong to. I know that sounds silly but that dog was my best friend." He scratched Lucky's ears.

"Brookhaven's policy was eighteen and out. By the time I turned eighteen, I'd lived there most of my life. Like my father before me, I had no skills, no means of going to college. I had nowhere to go, so I joined the Army. Of course, it was only a matter of time before they caught up with me anyway. The war was in full swing and the military needed all the able bodies they could get. They taught me how to kill, and how to survive in the jungle, and they sent me to the South Pacific."

He pulled in another breath, as if summoning the courage to continue. "The worst of the conflict was over by then, but there were remnant groups of the Japanese forces. They started an uprising. Our orders were to squash it. We completed our mission and were on our way out. By then the native people had started burning their village. It was a horrible sight: fire, destruction, buildings and trees exploding all around us. Our orders were to march and not look back and believe me, that's exactly what I intended to do. But as we were leaving, this old woman came running up to me. I believe she was some sort of a witch, or a Shaman. She grabbed onto my shirt, asking me... *begging* me to help her. I couldn't understand her, didn't know what she wanted, so I tried to shove her away. I thought it was some sort of trick. But then I realized what she was asking me to do. Her house was on fire, and I looked in the window, and I saw this little face. A little boy. I knew that if I went in I would probably be shot, but I couldn't keep walking, Willy. I couldn't walk away and leave that child in there to die."

A tear fell from his eye and Willy gently brushed it away.

"I'd seen so much killing, taken so many lives... I guess it seemed like a way to a redeem myself, both in front of God and in my own eyes. So I went into the house and I pulled the child out. I don't even know if he was alive when I put him in the old woman's arms.

"She had a chain around her neck, and she took it off and gave it to me. On the end of the chain there was a medallion. She pressed it in my hands and uttered some sort of spell. I didn't understand it, didn't want the charm, but she wouldn't take it back.

"After that it was like I had some sort of shield around me, like nothing bad could touch me. Thousands of men were dying all around me and I came through the war without a scratch. They awarded me medals for bravery, but I wasn't brave." His voice dropped to a whisper. "I was cursed."

They sat in silence for a long time, neither having words to express their feelings.

"After the war ended I was right back where I started. With no place to go. Most of the GIs were flooding into the cities, looking for houses and jobs, places to settle with their new wives, raise their families. The government started offering rural farmlands cheaply under the GI Bill of Rights. I didn't want the noise and the congestion of the city. I wanted solitude, a place to sort myself out, so I bought this house and the twenty acres it sat on. I just wanted to put the war behind me, to forget. I didn't want the medals, or the old woman's charm, but they weren't the sort of things a man throws away. So I put them in a box and buried them on the edge of my property."

~ * ~

The confession knocked the breath from Willy's lungs. She was beginning to understand now.

"Shortly after I returned home, I got a letter from Brookhaven telling me that Lucky was barely hanging on. They said he was waiting for me, waiting for me to return so he could die. They were going to shoot him and they thought I'd want to come and say goodbye. He'd been a good friend, and he deserved better than a bullet in the head, so I went to the farm and brought him back here to die. But he didn't die,

Willy. He got better.

"I got a job in the city, at the flour mill. A bunch of us used to commute together every day, mostly war vets. We'd get together on Saturday nights, play cards, re-hash the war. They were good men, good friends. For ten years I worked side by side with them, but then I started to realize something strange was happening. The years were passing me by, but I wasn't aging. Not like the other men. People started to comment on it, joked that I had a fountain of youth tucked away on my property. I couldn't explain it, but I knew it had something to do with the medallion. All I could think was that I'd buried the old woman's blessing with the charm and the land had become enchanted. A place where nothing would ever grow old or die. I realized I'd have to be careful, keep a low profile, so I quit my job and built the cabin. I rented out the cottage and saved the money, knowing it would have to last me for an eternity.

"The years came and they went. The world started to change. After awhile I couldn't keep up anymore and didn't want to try. I avoided going to town, afraid for people to see me. I lived off my land and bought what I needed in the city, where nobody knew me. When enough years passed, I told people I was Darby Sullivan's son. And then more years passed, and I became his grandson.

"I was blessed with the gift of life, but I felt cheated. I wanted a family, a wife and children. Then I met a woman and I allowed myself to believe my dreams could come true."

"Marilyn," Willy murmured.

"Yes. Marilyn. I tried to keep the truth from her but she eventually found out. She couldn't love me after she knew the truth. I can't say I blame her. What woman could?"

The silence was deafening, as if all of nature held its breath, waiting, until Willy's hands once again reached out and covered his. "I could."

~ * ~

He fought to control the tears that welled up in his eyes, the deep, wrenching sob that had lodged in his chest with the utterance of her words. Words he'd waited his entire lifetime to hear. She came to him and wrapped her arms around him, held him as though she'd never let him go.

"Whatever comes, Darby, we'll face it together."

"Willy, think about what you're saying. Even if by some miracle we were able to hold on to this land, it would never be the same. We'd be surrounded by swimming pools, hiking trails... people. I can't live like that. It would only be a matter of time before someone caught on. I'd become a freak, some sort of science experiment. I'd sooner die."

"Then we'll sell them the land. We'll take the money and start over again, someplace new. We'll dig up the medallion and take it with us. Maybe there's enough magic left--"

"No."

"Darby..."

"Maybe there's enough magic left, Willy, but maybe there isn't. If this land can heal Lucky, then it can heal you, too. As long as you stay here you'll be all right. If you leave, you might not be, and that's not a chance I'm willing to take."

"What are you saying, then?"

He sighed. "I'm saying we have to find a way for you to stay."

"And what about you?"

He didn't answer.

"Do you really think I'd stay here without you?" He heard anger in her voice, saw it in her eyes.

"Willy, I've lived a lot of years, I--"

"I've lived a few years, too, Darby, and not many of them have been happy ones. Life has given us both another chance. *Love* has given us another chance. If it comes down to dying or living without you, then I'd rather die."

Wrapped in her embrace, Darby felt a faint glimmer of hope. It stemmed more from the fact that she was willing to try, to love him, than of any faith in divine providence. He'd grown weary of hiding, of concealing the truth. Weary of life. But now this woman, this beautiful, gentle woman, was offering him a chance at love and hope for a future. He wasn't naïve enough to believe in fairy tales, in happily-ever-after, not where love was concerned, but consequences be damned, for Willy's sake, he had to try.

"All right. Then we'll fight them. Maybe if we meet them halfway, negotiate for the cottage and a couple of acres, and sell them the rest for their park..."

"We're going to need documents, papers naming you as your grandfather's legal power of attorney. You'll need a new birth certificate and Social Security number."

She was determined now, full of fight. He heard optimism in her voice and the glimmer of hope inside him sparked into a flame.

"How can we get those things, Willy?"

"There are people."

"People?"

"It's just a matter of finding them."

"How do we do that?"

She took a breath. "There are other people, Darby. Good people who can help us. But we have to tell them the truth."

"That would take an awful lot of trust."

"We can trust them, Darby. With our lives."

He thought about it and knew he had no choice. "I hope you're right," he said.

Seventeen

She was going to live.

All at once the world seemed a brighter place, a place filled with wonder and magic and countless possibilities. She would see another winter, know again December's quiet beauty and the childish pleasure of making angels in the snow. She would embrace the glory of autumn. She would know the satisfaction of raking leaves under a sailor blue sky and the smoky, woodsy scent of a crackling bonfire. She was going to live and it was all because of Darby.

For weeks she'd clung to a slim hope that she'd be cured. She'd begun to allow herself beautiful fantasies of a future at Darby's side. Now that her dreams were to become a reality, Willy didn't know whether to laugh or cry.

Her initial euphoria carried her through the day as she and Darby made cautious plans for a future she hadn't thought possible the day before. They walked hand in hand along the riverbank, dreaming together of a small, simple wedding in the garden, of children. Willy found herself wanting to shout for joy, while at the same time, she craved solitude, time and space in which to quietly ponder the twofold miracle that had occurred. Darby loved her, and she was going to survive the cancer. Together, they would live a fairy tale existence. Happily ever after.

Unless...

In the daylight all of their dreams had seemed possible, attainable. But now, in the dark of night, her fears crept in, torturing her with relentless whispers, telling her that none of it would happen. That their paradise was destined to become a public playground, equipped with picnic tables and ice cream stands. She felt tears coming and blinked them back. Surely fate wouldn't be so cruel, to give her a second chance at life and love, only to have it shattered with a blow from the Parks Commission's fist?

A larger fear surfaced, one she could not ignore. One that said that if by some miracle her wish was granted, her life spared, she would be a prisoner. She would attain life and love, but at what price?

Eternal youth.

She wrestled with images of she and Darby chained together in paradise forever. Life would go on all around them. The world would continue to change, evolve, and eventually, leave them behind. Would she, like Darby, come to see the blessing as a curse?

~ * ~

Her thoughts were heavy, and more than she could bear. She slipped out of bed, made her way quietly to the kitchen, and poured a glass of water. She carried it to the porch and stood looking out at the night, trying to sort out her feelings.

As if pulled from his sleep by her turbulent thoughts, Darby opened the screen door and came to stand beside her. "Are you all right?" he asked.

"I'm fine."

He wrapped his arms around her. She burrowed against his chest, taking comfort in the feel of his arms around her. She listened to the beating of his heart, and knew in that moment that no woman had ever loved a man more.

A coyote howled in the distance, a strange and mournful wail.

"Darby?"

"What, love?"

"What if the Parks Commission won't agree to a compromise?"

"Then we'll have to fight them."

"What if we lose?"

"Look at me." He tilted her face upward to meet his gaze. "Everything is going to be all right, Willy. I don't know how, but I promise you it will be."

~ * ~

Lying beside her, Darby thought of the lifetime of love he and Willy would share, pushing away frightening images of the enemy that lurked just beyond the gate. He'd made a promise, and he hoped to God he could keep it. He forced himself to breathe deeply, to relax. He would need a clear head tomorrow. He only hoped he had the courage to face what would have to be done, come morning.

Eighteen

Zoe Prescott was the embodiment of female ambition. A battered-wife-turned-lesbian, Zoe had recreated herself at age twenty-five. She returned to college, earned a law degree, and spent the next five years relentlessly crusading for downtrodden women. She'd taken some detours in life, but at thirty-five, Zoe felt that she'd finally arrived. She was at the top of her game, living life according to her own rules--a cyclone in the courtroom, highly respected by her peers and greatly feared by her enemies.

Sid had met her by a whim of fate two years before, at a Midtown Arts Festival. Sid volunteered to staff a booth where she and her co-workers had displayed their artwork in the hope of drumming up some business for the tattoo studio. Zoe had a particular liking for abstract body art and a soft spot for feisty brunettes, and both agreed it was love at first sight.

Willy had always felt put off by Zoe's abrupt personality, but she kept her thoughts to herself and did her best to maintain a positive relationship with Sid's new partner. When things fell apart with Tom, Zoe insisted on handling Willy's divorce pro bono. Willy had been and always would be grateful, but the thought of once again prevailing upon Zoe for her professional expertise tied her stomach in knots.

Knowing there was no way around it, she got up early and phoned Sid, asking if she and Zoe could come out to Baker's Gully as soon as possible.

"Can it wait until Saturday?" Sid asked sleepily.

"It's really important, Sid."

"All right, sit tight. Let me see what I can do."

Sid called her back within the hour, saying she'd found someone to cover her shift at the tattoo studio and that Zoe had a light day. "Hang tough, girlfriend," she said. "We'll be there in time for lunch."

As the four of them sat at the table in the dining room, Darby and Willy on one side, Sid and Zoe seated opposite them, Willy hoped she had made the right decision. With the lunch plates stacked in the sink, Willy poured four cups of coffee. Her hands trembled and her mouth felt as if it were full of cotton. She and Darby had decided to feel Zoe out about their chances of cutting a deal with the Parks Department before launching into the extraordinary details, but in the end, they'd have to make the truth known. Would Zoe believe them? And if so, would she help?

Though his face was impassive, Willy could feel Darby's apprehension as he explained his situation. Zoe listened intently, taking her eyes off Darby's face only to jot notes in her legal pad. When he'd finished speaking, Darby slid the hated letter across the table. Zoe studied it, a small frown creasing her brow. Finally she looked up.

"I won't lie to you, Darby, this isn't good. Cases like this can go either way. It could get real ugly before it's all said and done."

"They can force me to sell my land? Land that's been in my family for more than half a century?"

"I've seen it happen."

Darby's shoulders slumped.

"I don't suppose you have the original paperwork?"

Zoe asked. "From when the land was purchased?"

"I've got all of it in a safe," Darby said. "My grandfather bought the property cheaply under the GI Bill of Rights after the Second World War. It's worth four times what he paid for it, what they're offering."

Zoe brightened. "There might be a loophole there somewhere, some protective clause under the GI Bill. Provided the gentleman who bought the property is still alive?"

Darby pulled in a deep breath and Willy squeezed his hand under the table.

"He's still alive," he said.

"Great." Zoe scribbled furiously in her legal pad. "I'll look into it. We'll involve veterans' organizations if we have to. Maybe we can even put the old man in front of a television crew, garner some public support. Would it be possible for me to meet with him?"

Darby said nothing, and his prolonged silence caused Zoe to look up from her notes. He cleared his throat, and squarely met her gaze. "You're looking at him."

Zoe's expression was at first amused, then annoyed. "I thought you said the property was purchased in the 1940s?"

"It was."

Sid and Zoe exchanged glances, then Zoe folded her hands on the table in front of her. "Why don't you explain that to me, Darby?"

Slowly, falteringly, Darby did just that. He told her about Brookhaven and his military service. He told her about the old woman and the amulet, and how he buried it in the ground. When he was finished, both Sid and Zoe stared at him, speechless. Finally Sid ran her hands back through her hair. "Christ, Willy."

"What Darby says about the land is true," Willy said softly. "It has the power to heal. I'm living proof."

Zoe looked from Willy to Darby. "Incredible."

"Zoe, we're in a position to lose everything. Even our lives," Willy said. "We really need your help."

Zoe sat back in her chair and exhaled softly. "What is it you'd like me to do, Willy?"

"Take our case," Darby said. "Help us fight for what's rightfully ours."

Sid spoke up, her eyes and tone softly imploring. "What do you think, Zoe?"

"I think I could be disbarred for even considering it."

No one spoke for a long moment, until finally, Zoe slid the papers back across the table to Darby. "Sign here, on the line that says, *I do not* agree to these terms."

Darby signed his name on the document and Zoe tucked it into her briefcase. "This will stay on my desk until you can provide proof that you are your grandfather's legal power of attorney."

"How can I do that?" Darby asked.

Zoe sighed. "There are ways. None that I can condone, so you never heard this from me, understood?"

"Understood."

"I know a man, sort of a friend of a friend. He creates documents. He's very good at what he does, but he doesn't work cheap. In the past he's created new identities for battered women. I've looked the other way in the name of justice. What he does is highly illegal. But he's the best there is."

"How do I get in touch with him?" Darby asked.

"You don't." Zoe sighed again. "How much money have you got?"

"Money's not a problem," Darby told her.

"We'll get you what you need, Willy," Sid said, giving her a hug. "It might take awhile, but we'll get it."

"We've got twenty-eight days," Willy said softly.

"I'll do my best to stall them." Zoe stood and

gathered her papers. "Thanks for lunch. I'll be in touch."

They moved out to the front yard. Sid gave Willy another hug, then turned to Darby. "Take care of her."

~ * ~

The two weeks that followed were the best days Willy had ever known. She felt recharged, alive in every sense of the word. With heightened senses, she stood in awe of the earth around her, the way the flowers perfumed the air, the river embracing them like a crystal clear fountain as she and Darby laughed and played. Her nights were filled with a passion she couldn't have imagined possible. She was swept away in the joy of newfound love, and yet, the love she shared with Darby seemed ageless. She held him as he slept, as though trying to grasp hold of each, precious moment, and all the while a torturing voice whispered in her head that the clock was winding down... That she and Darby were running out of time.

Darby's fears echoed her own, one soft July morning. They walked the property line, planning, preparing for an altered way of life, should the Parks Department agree to their offer.

"This is where the property line would be, Willy," he told her, pointing out a row of sycamores. "We'd be left with only a fraction of what we have now."

She slid her arms around him. "It'll be enough."

~ * ~

"It's going to seem strange," he mused. "People coming and going all the time. This place has always been so secluded. That's one of the things I've always loved about it. I suppose they'll pave the road now, paint a yellow line down the center of it."

She held him close. "We'll build a privacy fence, surround it with evergreens and blue spruce. They won't even have to know we're here."

He faced her, his expression grave. "Are you

prepared to spend your life hiding, Willy? Live the life of a recluse? Friends will come and go. It'll never be safe to keep them for very long. No one will ever really know you. No one but me."

"You're all I want, Darby," she said, pressing her face into his chest. "All I'll ever need."

~ * ~

Willy went through her days with one her ear tuned to the phone as she anxiously waited for Sid's call. In the end, when the phone rang, it was Zoe's voice on the other end of the line.

"I received notification of your court date for the divorce," she said, getting right to the point. It was the last thing Willy expected to hear, and the news left her momentarily speechless.

"I thought that took months?" she finally said.

"It usually does, but money talks. Tom's lawyer pushed it to the head of the line. We're set for a week from today at nine a.m. Do you want to meet me here in the office, say eight- thirty?"

"I can do that."

"It shouldn't take too long. It's pretty much open and shut, so I'm guessing we'll be in and out in twenty minutes. And then, my dear, you will be free of Tom Mackenzie once and for all."

"Good. Thank you, Zoe. Thank you so much."

Zoe paused. "Regarding the other matter... those items you asked me to locate for you?"

Willy's heart constricted, and she found it hard to breathe. "Yes?"

"I've got them."

Nineteen

On the night before her scheduled court date, Willy lay beside Darby, basking in the pleasure his nearness brought her, and the love she could feel in every beat of his heart. Though Tom had professed his love daily, his words always seemed forced and perfunctory. Darby's love was fierce and quiet, tangible in the way he looked at her, in the way he spoke her name. She had never felt more connected to another human being, or more cherished. Darby Sullivan loved her, of that she had no doubt. Even so, something was troubling him. She sensed a sadness in him, an urgency in his lovemaking that she couldn't begin to guess the reason for.

"How long is this thing going to take, tomorrow?" he asked, stroking her hair.

"Not long. We're just tying up the loose ends. Twenty minutes, tops." She smiled in the darkness. "You can get along without me for a couple of hours, can't you?"

She'd been trying to lighten the solemn mood that seemed to have settled over him since he'd learned of Zoe's phone call, but her teasing remark only seemed to add to his distress.

"I don't want you to go, Willy," he said. "I don't have a good feeling about it."

She untangled herself from his embrace, propped herself on her elbow, and studied his face in the darkness. There was no mistaking the troubled expression in his eyes. "I have to go, Darby. I have to close the door on this marriage once and for all. And then we can move ahead with our plans." She kissed him lightly on the mouth. "This is a *good* thing. And besides, I want to talk to Zoe in person about our situation with the Parks Commission."

"Maybe I should go with you."

A part of her longed to agree, to have the comfort of Darby's presence with her in the courtroom, but the biggest part of her realized how selfish that would be. The trip to the city would take a toll on him, rob him of his vitality. It would age him.

"We've already been over this, Darby. We both agreed it would be better if you stayed here, remember?"

He sighed.

"It'll be all right. I promise."

~ * ~

Darby slept fitfully and awoke the next morning consumed by a fear he couldn't name. Dreams had come to him in the night: lightning flashes of images that his overworked brain could make no sense of. A young man in a red baseball cap turned backward. A silver sedan with a blood-soaked seat. Flashing red lights. Swirling gray fog and the overwhelming sensation that time was running out. He'd awakened soaked in sweat, his breath torn from his lungs in sharp, painful jags--terrified and not understanding why. Terrified, even in the light of a brand new day. The morning air was cool and pleasant, and the brightening sky promised a glorious, summer day. He sat across from Willy at the breakfast table, knowing her reasons for needing to go, knowing the dark clouds looming on the horizon were purely of his own imagining and, still, fighting the urge to beg her not to.

Stop being a jackass, Sullivan, he told himself. *She's just taking care of business. She'll be home by lunchtime.* But he couldn't seem to untie the knot of dread in the pit of his stomach, the terrible, nagging fear that told him he would never see her again.

"Call if anything comes up," he said, trying to keep his tone light. "I mean, if you're going to be delayed."

She smiled. "I will." She carried her dishes to the sink, grabbed up her purse, and returned to him, planting a kiss on his mouth. "I'll see you soon."

"Good luck."

"I won't need luck. I've got Zoe."

She tried to move away, but he held her fast. "I love you, Willy."

"I love you, too."

"If anything should happen, just try to get home, all right?"

"Darby, you're scaring me."

"I'm sorry," he said, and reluctantly let her go.

She kissed him again. "I'll see you soon."

He stood at the window and watched as her Explorer backed from the driveway and disappeared down the road, wrestling with a faceless enemy, an enemy he couldn't name, and therefore was powerless to fight.

~ * ~

By the time Willy reached the city limits, the temperature had climbed a full twenty degrees. She drove across town and parked in the lot beside Zoe's office building. Hot, stale air wrapped itself around her as she stepped from the comfort of her air- conditioned truck. She'd selected a lightweight blouse and matching skirt for the day, hoping to appear cool and unruffled, but she could already feel the fabric clinging to her back.

Zoe's waiting room was sleek and uncluttered, with crisp white walls offset by splashes of colorful artwork and voluptuous ferns perched on the oversized windowsills. It wasn't as imposing as the offices of Geoffrey Blye, but then, Zoe Prescott didn't need brass and leather accouterments to inspire confidence in her clients.

Willy stepped into the lobby where Bernice, Zoe's paralegal, fluttered about, tidying stacks of magazines in the waiting room and setting out stacks of Styrofoam cups for coffee.

"Good morning, Bernice," Willy greeted her. "Am I early?"

"You're right on time," she said with a smile. "Go on back, hon, Zoe's waiting for you."

Willy walked down the corridor to Zoe's private office. Zoe was seated behind her desk, studying a packet of paperwork. She glanced up when Willy entered. "Morning, kiddo. I'm just making a last run through these documents. Everything looks fine. Except you signed off on the 401K?"

"Yeah," Willy said meekly.

A frown dipped the corners of Zoe's mouth. "I wish you hadn't done that."

"I didn't think I'd need it. Considering the circumstances."

"Okay." Zoe sighed. "But we're going to hang tough on the spousal support issue. That bastard owes you."

"All right."

"Of course that will change if you and Darby should decide to get married, but we'll talk about that situation a little bit later." She shoved the paperwork into her briefcase and glanced at her watch. "Are you ready?"

~ * ~

The Torrence County Courthouse stood in the center of Courthouse Square, an immense configuration of stone walls and Gothic columns, with a domed roof of polished gold that seemed to reach up into the sky. Willy had always felt in awe of the two-hundred-year-old structure, feeling a strange reverence for this machine in which the wheels of justice continually turned.

Inside, she and Zoe took their places in line, where two armed security guards shepherded the morning flock of attorneys and their clients through a metal detector.

"Purse."

Startled by his sharp tone, Willy looked into the steely blue eyes of a security guard. "Excuse me?"

"He needs your purse," Zoe told her.

"Oh." Willy unhitched her bag from her shoulder and handed it to the guard, who placed it in a basket and onto a conveyor belt, where it underwent the scrutiny of an X-ray machine. She stepped through the electronic doorway to find it waiting for her on the other side.

"They're pretty uptight here," she commented to Zoe.

"Everyone's uptight since the thing in Oklahoma City," Zoe told her. "And nine-eleven certainly didn't help. Better safe than sorry, I guess."

She followed Zoe into the courtroom and took a seat near the front. Despite the early hour, the heat inside was oppressive. Within moments, Willy was overtaken by an uncomfortable wave of dizziness.

"How are you doing?" Zoe asked. "You okay?"

"Is it me, or is it really warm in here?" Willy asked, fanning her face with her hand.

"It's not you," Zoe grumbled. "With all the money they constantly dump into this place, you'd think they could keep the air conditioning running properly. At least we're one of the first cases on the docket."

~ * ~

Willy glanced around and spotted Tom sitting alone on the other side of the room. He lifted his hand in greeting, and Willy acknowledged him with a slight nod of her head. It amazed her that seeing him didn't hurt anymore, that she no longer ached to rush into his arms, to have him stroke her hair and tell her everything would be all right. Tom, with his expensive suit and his perfect haircut and the slight look of annoyance that was never far from his face. She thought of Darby, beautiful and untamed, and offered up a small prayer of thanks for him, and for the life they would soon begin together.

A bailiff entered the room, scattering her thoughts.

"All rise for the honorable Judge Bennett."

Judge Elsworth Bennett entered the courtroom, looking like Willy had always imagined a judge would, with his silver hair and his proud demeanor. He called the first case and listened as each attorney in turn presented their arguments. He was wise and stern, imposing despite his small stature, and Willy's stomach cartwheeled at the thought of approaching his bench.

Zoe leaned in and whispered, "I wonder where Blye is? We're supposed to be next."

When Judge Bennett called their case, Zoe approached his bench. Willy saw a look of annoyance flicker across his face, then he nodded and Zoe returned.

"He'd better get here soon," she said, resuming her seat, "or Bennett will push us back to the end of the line."

A half hour later, Zoe leaned in again. "I'm going to go and make a call, see if I can find out what's going on." She peered into Willy's face. "Are you all right?"

Willy's throat was parched, her head, pounding. "I don't know, Zoe."

"Sit tight. I'll bring you a glass of water."

Willy tried to focus on what was going on around her, but soon gave up caring and concentrated instead on taking slow, deep breaths. She was drenched in sweat, her heart pounding. When Zoe returned with a glass of water, she retrieved two painkillers from her purse and swallowed them.

"I couldn't get a straight answer out of Blye's secretary," Zoe told her. "This is highly unusual, to say the least."

By that time Willy was having trouble breathing. She longed to put her head between her knees but forced herself to remain upright. She watched with a detached sense of curiosity as the bailiff approached the bench and handed Judge Bennett a folded sheet of paper. He read it, then once again called for Zoe to approach the bench. He murmured softly to her, and when Zoe returned again, her face was colorless.

"What is it, Zoe?" Willy asked. "What's wrong?"

Zoe pushed out a breath. "It's not happening today."

Willy looked at her in alarm. "Not at all?"

"Blye is dead. They found him stabbed to death in his car in the parking garage. *Christ!* Let's get out of here."

Willy tried to stand but found her legs wouldn't support her. Zoe motioned for the bailiff, and the two helped Willy to her feet, supporting her as she stumbled from the courtroom. The air outside was ferocious. Willy sank onto a nearby bench, certain she would faint.

"What's happening, Willy?" Zoe asked, concern etching her face.

"The pain killers make me a little bit sick to my stomach," Willy replied, trying to catch her breath. "I know better than to take them on an empty stomach. I'll be all right in a few minutes."

"There's a café a couple of blocks from here. It's air-conditioned. Do you think you can walk now?"

~ * ~

Boomer's was crowded, despite the early hour. Secretaries and cops chatted together at the tables, while girls in crisp, red-and-white aprons scurried about behind the counter, filling orders for coffee and doughnuts. The cheerful chatter made Willy's head spin, but the cool air inside was a welcome relief. Zoe steered her to an empty table near the back and carelessly swept a clutter of crumbs and discarded doughnut wrappers onto the floor.

"Sit down, babe. God, you don't look good at all."

A waitress scurried over, and Zoe ordered a cup of herbal tea for herself, and toast for Willy. She fished her cell phone out of her bag and flipped it open. "Listen, I'm due back in court. I'm going to call Sid, see if she can come and sit with you until you're feeling better."

Too weak to protest, Willy nodded, feeling strangely disconnected as Zoe talked into her phone. She picked up a slice of toast but found herself unable to chew. Zoe's voice faded in and out, and the room became a disjointed kaleidoscope of colors and sounds around her. She felt desperate to be with Darby, to be safe in his arms.

Fifteen minutes later Sid walked into the café. Spotting Zoe and Willy at their table near the back, she hurried over. She slung her purse down into the booth and slid in across from Willy. A glance at Willy's face chased away her smile.

"Hey, girlfriend. You all right?"

The concern in her best friend's eyes was the last thing Willy saw before the room folded in on her and everything faded away to gray.

~ * ~

Darby spent the morning occupying himself with odd jobs around the cottage. He repaired the leaky kitchen faucet and replaced the ballast in the overhead light. As hard as he tried to keep his mind off of Willy, he found his eyes returning to the clock again and again. He counted the minutes and the hours as they ticked past and tried to calculate where Willy might be at any given moment. Fear clawed at his gut, until at last paralyzed by it, he sank down in a chair beside the telephone to wait. When it finally rang, at a quarter to eleven, it was almost a relief. He let it ring three times, then, bracing himself, he picked it up.

"Hello?"

"Darby?"

Hearing the choked, desperate sound of Sid's voice, he went numb. "What's wrong, Sid?"

He heard her shaky intake of breath. All time seemed to stop as he waited for her response. "Darby, something's wrong with Willy. We were having breakfast in the café and she... she blacked out."

He felt his heart constrict. He wanted to scream but forced his voice to remain calm. "Sid, listen to me. You need to bring Willy home. Right now."

"I can't," she choked out. "The ambulance came and took her to Fairview Hospital. Darby, she stopped breathing."

All of the anguish of a lifetime boiled up to the surface until Darby couldn't breathe either. "Where is she now?"

"She's in the ER examining room. I'm right outside the door."

"Stay with her, Sid. Whatever you do, do not leave her alone. I'm on my way."

Twenty

Mass-produced for the military in 1941, the Willys Jeep proved a solid, dependable work vehicle. When the war ended, the truck's rugged durability made it a popular choice for the average working man. It was built to last, if not built for speed. Normally, Darby was content to crawl, but today, every mile seemed an eternity as he crept toward the city, toward the woman who needed him, the woman he loved.

He kept his eyes firmly fixed on the road ahead, but his thoughts wandered aimlessly through the vast wasteland of his past. Every loss and every bitter disappointment he had ever known was revisited. Nothing in his entire life experience had caused him more pain than the thought of losing Willy, and though he had never been a particularly religious man, Darby found himself praying.

Please, God... If You're there... Please...

When he finally entered the city limits, he gazed around him, only mildly interested in the changes that had taken place since he'd last been. The main thoroughfare, which had formerly consisted of two lanes bustling with businessmen in Packards and women out shopping in Plymouth Suburban wagons, had swelled to four lanes of bumper-to-bumper traffic. Look-alike plazas, busy with neon, had replaced the quiet, mom and pop businesses along

Lexington Avenue. Boys lounged on the street corners, wearing oversized blue jeans and silver rings in their eyebrows, while girls strolled the sidewalks, barely dressed.

He followed the signs for Fairview Hospital and drove into the vast, crowded parking lot. He circled the perimeter three times, cursing each wasted moment, and finally lumbered into a parking garage, jamming the truck into the first empty space he saw.

The hospital was immense, a color-coded labyrinth of corridors and locked doors and dead end hallways. He located the Emergency Room entrance and hurried up to the horseshoe-shaped desk, where a nurse sat, talking on the telephone. He shifted impatiently from foot to foot, waiting for her attention. On the wall behind her, the clock ticked on, valuable moments slipping away. Would there be no end to the woman's incessant chatter?

"Excuse me," he said loudly.

With a glance that conveyed annoyance, she held up a finger, signaling him to wait. But Darby couldn't wait. Another nurse hurried past, and he sprinted after her and planted himself directly in her path.

~ * ~

"Please. I'm looking for Willow Mackenzie. She was brought here by ambulance more than an hour ago."

"I remember her," the nurse said. Her expression contained a mix of pity and sadness that told Darby the situation was dire. "She's been taken up to ICU, honey."

"How do I get there?"

She directed him to a bank of green elevators, instructing him to take them to the fourth floor. He thanked her, then turned and bolted down the corridor. Finding the green elevators, he waited for the doors to open, then jostled his way inside. When the doors slid open on the fourth floor, he pushed his way into the lobby and frantically looked around.

"Can I help you with something?"

Another nurse sat at another horseshoe-shaped desk. He approached her and repeated his request.

"Yes, Willow Mackenzie was admitted twenty minutes ago. Only immediate family is permitted inside. Her sister's with her now."

"I'm her fiancé."

Sympathy hovered in her eyes for a moment then disappeared.

"All right."

She directed him to a set of double doors, where a sign read: *Push Button and Wait for Nurse to Respond.*

He pushed the button. Peering through the small rectangle of glass, he saw sterile white walls lined with metal gurneys and medical equipment, and several white doors, all of them closed. He pushed the button again. Finally, a nurse appeared, and her voice crackled through the intercom.

"Yes?"

"I'd like to see Willow Mackenzie. I'm her fiancé."

The doors slid open, a heavyset nurse with a bulldog face on the other side. "Come with me."

He followed her down the white corridor and stood back while she opened the third white door on her left. Darby stepped inside, bracing himself for the worst. Nothing could have prepared him for the knife blade of pain that tore through his chest at the sight of Willy.

She lay in a hospital bed, looking small and pale and lost amid the array of medical equipment that surrounded her. Her eyes were closed, and he approached quietly and gently brushed her cheek with his hand.

"Oh, Darby. Thank God you're here." Sid sat in a chair beside the bed, looking as forlorn and wrung out as Darby felt. Black mascara streaked her face.

"What happened, Sid?"

"We thought the heat had gotten to her, but the

doctor says she blacked out from pain." Sid drew a shaky breath. "The tumor is pressing against her brain. Darby, she's bleeding inside."

"We've got to get her out of here."

~ * ~

The nurse stared at him, incredulous. "Oh, that's out of the question. All of this equipment might look intimidating but it's what's keeping her alive. She'd die before you got out of the parking lot."

The heartless comment did Sid in, and the room filled with the sound of strangled sobs. Darby leaned in close to Willy and softly stroked her hair.

"It's going to be all right, darlin'," he murmured.

"She probably can't hear you," the nurse said. "She's in a drug-induced coma. We had to do it in order to keep her calm and comfortable."

Darby's anger flared again. He wanted to lash out, to hurt as he was hurting. *Easy,* he told himself. *Hold your temper. There's no point in getting yourself kicked out.*

"You can leave now," he said curtly. "I'm sure you have work to do. We'll call you if we need anything."

The nurse stared at him for a long moment before turning on her heel and marching from the room.

"I'd like to be alone with her if you don't mind," he told Sid.

"All right." She bent and kissed Willy's cheek. "You'll call me? If anything should happen?"

"Nothing's going to happen."

Sid took a last, longing look at her friend, squeezed Darby's shoulder, and quietly slipped from the room. Darby sank into the chair beside the bed and cautiously reached for Willy's hand. He gazed at her pale, beautiful face and saw his life stretching out ahead, a succession of endless, empty days and moments and hours. Tears he no longer fought to control streamed down his face.

"I'm not going to let you die, Willy." She went on sleeping, and his voice dropped to a strangled whisper. "Willy, please. Come back to me."

~ * ~

Willy, please come back to me...

The voice of her lover flooded Willy's senses, and a warm, comforting glow washed over her, momentarily distracting her from her dream. She hovered for a moment on the precipice between conscious and unconscious thought, knowing that he lay somewhere just beyond the swirling gray fog that enveloped her. His words and the love that radiated from his voice beckoned to her like a lighthouse. She tried to concentrate on its steady beam, but the effort of finding her way through the swirling mist was too much, and she slid back down inside herself, until once again, she was alone.

It seemed like hours had passed since Grandma and Buss had left her alone in the parking lot. Her wide eyes strained toward the windows of the restaurant, hoping to catch a glimpse of them. Above her head and all around her, the air was becoming dark. A storm was coming and Willy felt afraid.

She clutched the pieces of her broken sand dollar as if they might offer her some protection from the storm. She bit her lip, trying not to cry, as she painstakingly sought to fit the pieces back together. But like the broken pieces of her life, the sand dollar was beyond repair, and she wept.

~ * ~

Willy... Can you hear me? I'm going to make everything all right. I promise you that...

She looked up and saw a face, the face of the man who loved her. He reached out his hands, strong, callused hands, and she placed the broken pieces inside them.

Big, callused, beautiful hands, they closed around the fragments. She gazed into his eyes, and knew that no one ever had, or ever would, love her more.

Her eyes were drawn back to his hands, which were opening slowly. Her breath caught as a small, white head emerged, followed by the body of a dove, whole and strong. She reached out trembling fingers to stroke its lovely feathers. The man lifted his hands in the air, and the dove flew away, her soft cries echoing down from the heavens.

I'm going to get you out of here, Willy...

He smiled at her and once again extended his hand. Reaching out, she felt it close around hers. Clutching it like a lifeline, she held fast to her lover's hand and walked with him. She was sheltered in his love, safe from the coming storm...

~ * ~

Darby sat beside Willy's bed for the remainder of the afternoon. He couldn't stop touching her, talking to her, staring at the monitors that surrounded her, as if they held some sort of answers. Fatigue crept around the corners of his brain, and an aching weariness seeped into his bones, until finally, exhaustion overtook him and he slept.

He awoke hours later, his muscles cramped and knotted. The darkening sky outside the window told him he'd slept far longer than he intended. His eyes shot to Willy's face then traveled to the monitor above her head. The lines still zigzagged across the screen, and Darby took a small measure of comfort in this, though he couldn't begin to guess what it meant.

The room had become chilly while he slept, and he reached out to tuck Willy's blanket closer around her. The door opened and a nurse walked in. She stared at him in disbelief. "How did you get in here?"

"A nurse let me in."

"I've been here since two o'clock. I didn't see you come in." She glanced around the room. "Where's the other gentleman?"

Darby stared at her. "Other gentleman?"

"Willow's fiancé. Last I was in here he was asleep in the chair."

Darby realized with a sickening sensation what was happening, and vaguely wondered how far it had progressed, how many years had slipped away while he slept.

"He had to leave. This is my shift."

"Well, your shift is over, my dear. Visiting hours ended thirty minutes ago." She fiddled with the monitor above Willy's head, scribbled a note in Willy's chart, and replaced the clipboard in its slot on the wall.

Darby was afraid to ask, but more afraid not to. "How's she doing?"

The nurse gave him a long look, as if deciding, then said, "Not good. She's bleeding, and the pressure is building on her brain. We'll keep draining off the excess fluid, but it's only a matter of time. Listen, you look exhausted. Why don't you go home and get some rest? You're going to need it."

Under the nurse's watchful eye, Darby placed a tender kiss on Willy's forehead. "I have to leave now, Willy. Sleep well."

Outside Willy's room, the corridor was dark and quiet. Seeing a men's room at the end of the hallway, Darby opened the door and went inside. He used the urinal, then walked over to the sink and washed his hands, careful to avoid the mirror. He let the water run cold and doused his face, hoping it would clear his head. Bracing himself, he opened his eyes and looked into the mirror.

A man of fifty-five stared back at him. His hair was more silver than brown, and patches of gray peppered the stubble on his chin. His eyes were sorrowful, the soulful, weary eyes of a man who had seen too much.

Darby slowly released his breath. He'd aged twenty-five years in a day, and couldn't imagine what was happening inside of Willy. He'd come here with the intention of somehow smuggling her out, but he could see now that it wasn't going to be possible. Her room was on the fourth floor, with the window overlooking the hospital entrance. Besides that, any removal or tampering with the equipment she was hooked up to would immediately alert the nurses. He walked from the hospital, a broken man. There was only one thing left to do, and the thought of it broke his heart.

Out in the parking garage, the Willys choked and sputtered, refusing to start. Retrieving a pair of jumper cables from the back, Darby scoured the garage in search of a Good Samaritan. After receiving a jump start from a young man in a beat-up Ford Escort, he drove from the garage, feeling like Cinderella at the midnight hour. He prayed he wouldn't run out of time.

Home at last, he stepped wearily from the truck. Lucky padded out to meet him, his gaze moving past Darby to the truck.

"She's not with me, boy," Darby said, patting the dog's head. With a swish of his tail, the dog followed Darby into the house, where he retrieved a pen and a sheet of notepaper from his desk. Striking a match, he lit the wick of a kerosene lantern and carried the items to the porch. In the soft glow of firelight, he poured the contents of his heart onto paper, sealed up the envelope, and set it aside.

With a heavy heart, he walked to the shed, retrieved a shovel and a flashlight, and took them to the edge of his property, to the place he had discreetly marked with stones. The atmosphere was charged, and the hair on his arms stood on end.

The earth shuddered beneath his feet as he drove the shovel into the dirt. With the urgency of a man running out of time, Darby plunged the shovel, again and again, into the ground. He dug furiously in the moonlight, the air around him still, as the forest held its breath, waiting. Waiting, not a sound to be heard except for the soft thump of earth being torn away, until at last, he heard the unmistakable chink of metal on metal.

He lowered himself into the hole. Brushing away the remaining dirt with his hands, he lifted out the box.

Twenty One

She couldn't feel him anymore.

Panic-stricken, Willy stumbled through the fog, throwing terrified glances left and right, like a small child who has lost her way.

Darby? Where are you?

She stopped to listen, but hearing no answer, stumbled on.

The atmosphere was cool and damp and impenetrable. Where had he gone? How had she lost hold of his hand? Hearing a distant rumbling in the air, she stopped again to listen. Beyond the thick wall of whiteness she could hear the vague sounds of murmuring voices, words she couldn't decipher.

Darby?

A glaring light broke through the fog, and cold, rough hands touched her; but they were not his hands, and she struck out at them, flailing like a frightened animal.

~ * ~

All at once pain tore through her skin, a searing, stinging heat. The light and the voices faded away and Willy was left alone in the mist, weeping, calling for her lover...

~ * ~

It was after midnight when Darby carried the box

into the cabin. With hands that wouldn't stop shaking, he opened the clasp and carefully pushed away the layers of paper he'd placed inside so many years ago. The medallion glinted up at him, glowing in the soft flame of the lantern on the table beside him. Pushing out a breath, he reached for it, lifted it out, and held it in his hand. An electrical charge shot through him, making his skin tingle, telling him all he needed to know. He carefully wrapped it in paper and placed it back inside the box.

He moved to the mirror and surveyed again the damage time had wrought. The day in the city had aged him at least twenty years. Could she still love him? No longer able to fight off his fatigue and the questions that tormented him, he lay across his bed and allowed his body a few precious hours of sleep in which to recover.

He awoke at five a.m., exhausted but determined. He showered quickly, dressed in yesterday's clothes, and set out. Stepping onto the porch, he allowed his gaze to sweep across the landscape, taking in every detail, knowing it would never look quite the same again.

He reached the hospital at eight o'clock, went directly to the ICU, and pressed the buzzer beside the double doors. They slid open, revealing a male nurse with a dark crew cut and an easy smile. "What can I do for you?" he asked.

"I'm here to see Willow Mackenzie. I know it's early..."

"Not a problem."

He entered the room and was surprised to find Sid already there. She glanced up at him and her expression of curiosity quickly became one of shocked recognition.

"Good morning, Sid," he said.

"Hello... Darby." His name died on her lips as she stared into his eyes.

Darby's gaze went directly to Willy and he was

dismayed to see that she looked worse this morning than she had the night before. Her skin was milky white, and her breathing, labored.

"How is she doing today?" he asked.

"Slightly better," the nurse said. "We almost lost her in the night. Her heart rate shot up, and she became very agitated. Kept calling for her fiancé. At least she's stable again." He took a moment to adjust the IV bag beside Willy's bed. When he was satisfied with it, he turned back to Darby. "Her doctor will be in this morning to see her. He'll also want to talk to her family, discuss their options." He turned and walked from the room, his words hanging heavy in the air behind him.

Sid's eyes flew back to Darby's face, drinking in every detail. "Darby, what's happening to you?" she whispered.

"Don't worry about me, Sid."

Her eyes wandered back to Willy's face and filled with tears. "You know what the doctor wants to discuss with us, what he's going to recommend. What our so-called options are."

"We don't need his options." He pulled the medallion from his pocket and showed it to her. "We have this."

Sid gasped softly. "Is that...?"

"Yeah."

Tears spilled from her eyes and onto her cheeks. "Oh my God."

"Why don't you go and get a cup of coffee?"

"All right."

Darby followed Sid to the door and looked out. Scanning the length of the hallway, he saw the male nurse and two others congregated around the desk, talking softly as they swallowed coffee from Styrofoam cups. Heart pounding, he closed the door and returned to Willy's side.

He gently lifted her head, being careful not to upset the oxygen tube that was taped beneath her nose. Cradling her head in his hands, he pressed the medallion against the base of her skull. "Willy, can you hear me?" he asked. "Everything's going to be all right, darling. Just try to hold on."

In the interlude before sleep, he'd tried to tell himself his age wouldn't matter, that he and Willy could still go on as planned. But in the cold light of morning he'd seen the truth in Sid's eyes. He was an old man, and Willy, a beautiful butterfly. He wanted her to soar, to live her life freely and fully. He would be a hindrance, an obstacle, eternally blocking her flight. Bowing his head, he closed his eyes and concentrated, breathing deeply, emptying his mind of all conscious thought. He allowed himself to drift back in time to the old woman, willed himself to hear again the words she'd spoken. Slowly, falteringly, he repeated the words he could not understand, but that were deeply engraved on his heart. His entire body shuddered as the blessing departed from him. He sat back, sweating, utterly spent. It was done.

Sid returned a half hour later, carrying two steaming cups of coffee. She handed one to Darby. "You look like you could use this."

"Sid, I have to leave now."

A look of concern crossed her face. "Why?"

He was achingly tired, each word an effort. "Listen to me carefully, Sid. I need you to sit here, next to her. I need you to hold the medallion close to her head. Keep it near her at all times, no matter what, understand?"

Sid set down the coffee cups and moved in close. "All right."

"Whatever you do, do not leave her alone."

"All right, Darby."

She held out her hand, and Darby paced the

medallion in her palm. "If I don't make it back here, tell her..." His voice cracked. "Tell her I love her very much."

"Where are you going?" Sid asked.

Not answering, he leaned over and gave Willy one last kiss, one last whispered, "I love you," and quietly slipped from the room.

Knowing time was dangerously short, he hurried to the parking garage, started the truck, and pulled out onto the street. His breathing was labored, and tears blurred his vision. As the miles rolled slowly past, long-ago memories stirred before his eyes.

Why do I have to go away, Mama?

Be a good boy now, Darby. It's only for a little while.

His mother knelt at his side and kissed him. Even now, he could feel the soft brush of her dress and smell her faint, sweet perfume. He clung to her, knowing as only child can know that he would never see her again...

A sob lodged in his chest. He ached to pull the truck over, to rest his tired eyes, to be free of the pain of living and of losing. But not here. Not now.

Rattling down the interstate, he was helpless to stop the pictures from rolling across his mind.

Know what I miss the most, Sully? Besides Carolyn?

What's that?

I miss my grandmother's pie. Swear to God it was six inches thick. First thing I'm gonna do when this is all over, I'm gonna sink my teeth into one of those pies.

Darby smiled. *Sounds good.*

You should think about coming to Indiana, after the war. My uncle can get us both jobs in his store. I'll introduce you around to Carolyn's friends.

He couldn't see Joe's face in the darkness, but Darby took comfort in the sound of his voice, and the soft glow of his cigarette in the night, until the barely perceptible sound of snapping twigs put him them both instantly on the alert. *You hear that?*

~ * ~

What do you suppose it wa--

Before Joe finished speaking, Darby saw the flash of gunfire. He felt a searing pain in his shoulder, then the pressure of dead weight against him as Joe Barker fell into his arms. Joe Barker, his comrade, his friend. One moment, happy in his memories, and the next, gone forever.

"Oh, God, please... " Darby choked out. "I can't bear it."

He squeezed his eyes shut against the pain, but the memories kept coming. His mother. Joe Barker. Marilyn. All people he'd loved, pieces of his life, tragically lost.

At last his tortured thoughts turned to Willy. Willy, with her beautiful smile, and her voice, as soft as silk, whenever she said his name. He considered the days and the weeks and the years that added up to a man's life, the pros and the cons, the victories and the losses. The losses could be devastating, even staggering, but sometimes in the losing, something much, much larger was gained.

Maybe the measure of a man's existence was not in the years he spent on earth, but in the love those years contained. If that was the case, then he could go to his grave knowing his life had been worthwhile, because so beautiful a creature as Willow Mackenzie had loved him.

By the time he reached Murphy's Crossing his sight had grown dim, and his hands were gnarled and liver-spotted on the steering wheel. Four miles up Baker's Gully Road, the truck sputtered and died. Leaving it on the shoulder, he began to walk, his steps slow and painful.

~ * ~

When he reached Willy's cottage, he stopped to rest. His eyes moved over the yard. It had a forlorn, empty look. Brown patches dotted the lawn and the flowers were not as vivid as they had been that morning.

Retrieving a fallen tree branch from beside the road to use as a walking stick, he continued on toward home. Halfway up the path, Lucky hobbled out to greet him. His coat was gray, and his eyes, pale and watery. Darby eased himself to a squat and buried his face in Lucky's neck. He spoke, and his voice was the voice of a very old man.

"Were you waiting for me? Well, I've made it. I've made it."

Hearing his master's voice, Lucky wagged the tip of his tail, and Darby smiled.

"We had a hell of a run, didn't we, boy?"

The dog answered with a low howling sound and a soft nuzzling of Darby's hand. Using the branch for support, he dragged his body upright. Every muscle screamed in protest. He steadied himself, then gave the dog a last pat on the head.

"Come on, boy. Let's go home."

Twenty Two

For the next four days Willy slid in and out of consciousness. Sealed within a hazy, dreamlike existence, it was a struggle to open her eyes, to hold onto a conscious thought. Sometimes she surfaced to find Sid sitting at her bedside. Other times it was Zoe's face she saw, and though it gave her comfort to know her friends were near, Willy felt lost and increasingly frightened. Where was Darby? She fought to throw off the lethargy that smothered her like a blanket, but found she was unable to move her arms and legs, or even to speak.

Days passed and Willy was aware of little more than daylight turning to darkness, then returning again outside her window. There were more people, more unfamiliar faces at her bedside: doctors and medical students and nurses continually prodding, probing, running batteries of tests, seeking scientific reasons for the miracle that seemed to be occurring inside her. One by one, pieces of machinery were unhooked and removed, and little by little, Willy was weaned off the medications that kept her calm, but incoherent.

On the tenth day, Willy awoke to a bright, summer sky outside her window.

She felt healthy and lucid, as if all of her faculties

had been restored. She cautiously wiggled her fingers, then her toes. Everything seemed to be in good working order. Encouraged, she raised her hand in front of her face, made a fist, let it go.

"Oh, I see you're awake. Good then. How do you feel today?"

Startled by the nurse's abrupt appearance, Willy dropped her hand back to her side. Her throat was dry, and her voice rusty with disuse.

"I feel good."

"Excellent." The nurse started at Willy for a moment, as if she were an apparition, or a celebrity. "I came to help you get cleaned up. Today's moving day."

"Moving day?"

"We're moving you down to the second floor. Don't look upset, now. That's good news."

"Is Sid coming today?"

"Sid? Oh, your sister. Well, I imagine she'll be here before long. The poor girl has barely left your side in ten days."

Ten days. It seemed a lifetime since she'd seen Darby's smile, since she'd felt the comfort of his arms around her. "Has there been a man who came to visit me? A man with dark hair and gray eyes?"

A wrinkle creased the older woman's brow. "Well now, there have been a good many doctors in here, and no end to the medical students. I suppose some of them were dark-haired. Why do you ask?"

Swallowing her disappointment, Willy sank back into her pillows. "No reason."

"We're going to start you on a clear diet today, but breakfast will have to wait until later. They want you downstairs in thirty minutes for a brain scan. After that your new room should be ready for you."

She helped Willy out of bed and down the hallway

to a small, lime green bathroom, waiting outside the door while Willy used the toilet and brushed her teeth. She longed for a hot shower, but the nurse handed her a scratchy, white cloth, telling her a wash-up of face and hands would have to do for the time being. Back in Willy's room, the nurse combed Willy's hair and secured it with a rubber band.

"Okay, Madame," she said, pulling up a wheelchair. "Your chariot."

"I don't need a wheelchair," Willy protested. "I feel perfectly fine."

"Hospital policy," she said matter of factly. "Now sit. Oh, and you'll have to take off your necklace before you go in. How about if I take it now, and leave it at the front desk for you?"

"Necklace?" Willy placed a hand at her throat and felt a thin, unfamiliar chain, a small pendant attached to it. Curious, she undid the clasp, brought the pendant to her face, and studied it.

It was silver, the size of a quarter, etched with symbols and miniscule, foreign letters. It was smooth and warm, and she felt an inexplicable tingling sensation in her palm. A slow realization dawned as she stared at the medallion, recognizing it though she'd never laid eyes on it before. Her breath rushed from her chest, and she felt as if she'd faint. The medallion. The reason for the medical miracle.

But if the medallion was here with her, then--

"Oh," she cried softly. "Oh, no."

The nurse stared at her, a puzzled expression on her face. "Something wrong?"

Willy hurriedly rose from the chair. "I've got to get out of here."

"Hold on there, now." The nurse's arms shot out to restrain her. "What's got you so upset all of a sudden? You'll be leaving soon enough."

"You don't understand. I have to leave right now, immediately!" She struggled to free herself from the other woman's iron hold.

The nurse reached beside the bed and pressed the call button.

"Yes?" a voice crackled through the intercom.

"I've got an agitated little girl down here. I need help, stat!" She turned her attention back to Willy, her voice soothing, maddeningly condescending. "All right, missy. Help is on the way."

"You can't keep me here like this! Let me go!" She tried to pitch her body forward, but the nurse held her fast.

Moments later a doctor hurried into the room, Sid right behind him.

"Willy, my God. I heard you yelling all the way down the hall. What's going on?"

"You'll have to wait outside, Miss," the doctor told her.

"What's going on?" Sid repeated, peering past the doctor, who was closing in on Willy as if she were a wild animal.

"Sid, where's Darby?"

She saw a flash of pain in Sid's eyes.

"Where is he?"

"Willy... "

She saw the glint of a hypodermic needle in the doctor's hand. "All right, Willow. Everything is going to be just fine."

"You can't do this!" she shrieked. "Sid, call Zoe!"

The doctor jammed the needle into her arm, and she went tumbling back into the mist.

Twenty Three

Willy surfaced again hours later to find Sid sitting beside the bed, peering anxiously into her face. "Are you awake?" she asked.

"I think so. What time is it?"

"Almost two."

"Those bastards."

"I'm sorry, Willy. There was nothing I could do to stop them. But listen, Zoe paid the hospital administrator a little visit. You can leave whenever you want to."

"I want to." She sat and, momentarily overcome by a wave of dizziness, sank back into her pillows.

"Take it easy, babe," Sid soothed.

Willy closed her eyes, squeezing back sudden tears. "Sid, do you think he's all right?"

After a lengthy pause, Sid said, "I don't know."

"When was the last time you saw him?"

"Ten days ago."

"Oh, God." She placed a trembling hand to her lips. "Have you tried to call him?"

"A dozen times a day. He doesn't answer the phone."

Fear gripped Willy like a fist. She forced herself to breathe, to remain calm. Slowly, she pulled herself upright.

"Any idea where they stashed my clothes?"

"They're in my washing machine, but Zoe brought some things this morning."

Willy stood unsteadily to her feet, shed her hospital gown, and dressed in the black gauze skirt and matching top Sid offered.

"Okay," she said. "Let's get out of here."

~ * ~

Fifteen minutes later the hospital's head physician signed Willy's release papers. He did not look pleased. Willy thought him pompous and rude, and guessed that his displeasure stemmed from disappointment that she would no longer be readily available for testing, rather than a genuine concern for her well being. As though his favorite toy had been taken away.

"I must say, this is highly irregular," he said stiffly. "We were simply doing our jobs, and I certainly saw no reason for you to bring your lawyer in."

Willy said nothing as he scrawled his signature on the paperwork. "I would think being in such a fragile medical state, you'd want to stay, to have us--"

"To have you use me as a science experiment? No thank you."

"Ms. Mackenzie! If you'll forgive an observation, your current behavior is not only irrational, but very ungrateful, as well. We saved your life."

She knew it must seem that way, from his side of the desk. But she was too heartsick, too consumed with worry over Darby to care. "I apologize. And if the situation at home weren't so pressing--"

"I'm going to sign your release AMA," he said, interrupting. "And I'd like to see you again in two or three days, if it's not too much bother."

As she stepped outside the hospital and into the sunshine, Willy took a moment to fill her lungs with clean, fresh air, and to savor the feel of the sun on her face. She shaded her eyes with her hands and peered across the parking lot.

"Where's my truck?"

"You came by ambulance, remember?" Sid said.

"So where's my truck?"

"Ummm, it's at the Blue Lion. Chance's car has been in the shop, so he's been using it. I didn't think you'd mind."

"I don't," Willy said, but she was more than a little frustrated by the delay.

Sid made the trip across town in record time and pulled her Neon into the lot beside the Explorer. "Let me just run in and tell him," she said, getting out of the car.

"Sid, I want to go alone."

Sid gaped at her. "Are you crazy? You can't drive yet. Didn't you hear what they said?"

"Yes, I did. They said not to drive or operate heavy machinery. They said not to lift anything heavy, drink any alcohol, or eat anything besides Jell-O. Sid! Their rules don't apply, because their medicines and procedures are not what cured me." She dropped her voice and lifted the medallion from the front of her blouse. "This did, remember?"

Sid sighed. "I hate to have you go alone."

"Sweetie, I appreciate all you've done, all the time you sat with me. But I need to do this on my own." With a hug and a promise to call, Willy gunned the Explorer and pulled out into the street.

Driving home, Willy kept the windows all the way down, hoping the fresh air would dispel the lingering effects of the sedative. She raced down the interstate, her need for Darby making her drive faster than she normally dared. She was both impatient and terrified to reach Baker's Gully, to see what time had wrought. She prayed, and her plea consisted of one heartfelt word. *Please. Oh, please...*

When at last she turned onto Baker's Gully Road, she slowed the truck to forty miles per hour, but nothing could have tamed her galloping pulse. When she rounded the last bend and caught sight of the cottage, she cried out softly and hit the brakes. She sat for a long moment, staring. Tears gathered in her eyes and spilled down her cheeks.

The roses were dead.

~ * ~

The buds, magnificent ten days before, were now shriveled bits of faded pink encased in folds of brown. The vines, once lush and lovely, looked like small, coiled snakes, here and there parting to reveal weathered boards and peeling paint.

Her hands trembled on the wheel as she pulled into the driveway. She climbed from the Explorer and stood for a moment, gazing at the cottage. It had a desolate, deserted look, but it was more the acute sense of emptiness that filled her being that told her Darby wasn't there.

A noise drifted to her across the river, and she stood very still, listening. It came again. The distinctive *pound-pound-pound* of metal slamming against wood.

"Darby?" she whispered. Her heart leapt inside her and she turned and hurried down the path. Half walking, half running, she hurried toward him, her head and heart filled with all of the things she meant to tell him. When the foliage thinned and the cabin came into view, Willy saw an unfamiliar truck parked in the driveway. Her elation seeped out of her like air from a punctured tire when she discovered the source of the noise.

A man stood, his back to her. He wiped the sweat from his brow, then lifted his mallet and drove a posted sign into the ground. *Pound-pound-pound!* Other signs stood, queued like intermittent soldiers, across the property. *No Trespassing! Keep out by order of the NY State Parks Commission.*

She cried out softly, and the man turned his startled gaze her way. He was in his forties, powerfully built, with a kind smile that did little to ease her pain.

"Something I can help you with?"

"What... " Willy faltered, then somehow found her voice. "What are you doing here?"

"I might ask the same of you, Miss."

"This house belongs to my fiancé."

"It was my understanding that it belonged to the Parks Department."

The front door yawned open on its hinges and she shot a glance at the darkened doorway. "Where's Darby?"

"Darby? You mean the old man?"

"Darby Sullivan. The man who owns this property. Where is he?"

"He's gone, Miss," the man said, his tone softening. "Was found dead in his bed, oh, probably a week ago or more. He and his dog."

Willy's breath rushed from her lungs and she reached out blindly, grasping for one of the signs on which to steady herself. "What happened to him?"

"He got old, Miss. He got old and he came home to die. People do that sometimes."

Pain raged inside her, tearing ragged sobs from her breast.

"You all right, Miss? I'm awfully sorry you had to find out this way."

She turned and hurried back down the path. Tears blurred her vision and she stumbled and fell. She lay prostrate on the ground, weeping, crushed beneath the weight of a sorrow that would never ease. She was lost in a thick veil of darkness that would never lift, craving light from a sun that would never shine again.

~ * ~

It was early evening when she unlocked the back

door of the cottage and let herself inside. A closed-up, musty smell lingered in the air, as if the house had been empty for a decade, instead of less than two weeks. Emotionally drained, she set a kettle of water boiling on the stove for tea. Ignoring the flashing message light on her answering machine, she walked through the living room and into the bedroom.

She stripped off Zoe's skirt and blouse, which were torn and dirty from her fall, and opening her closet, pulled out a simple, white sundress. She was careful to avoid looking at the bed, the place she and Darby had been intimate, one of the last places she had seen him alive.

She combed her hair and pulled it back in a ponytail, then returned to the kitchen and removed the now shrieking teakettle from its burner. She made herself a slice of toast, then filled a cup with hot water, added a chamomile teabag, and carried it outside to the porch. She noticed an envelope lying on the floor beneath the table, as if displaced by a strong wind. Setting down her teacup, she bent to retrieve it. She turned it over and studied it. A current of pain rippled through her at the sight of her name scrolled across the envelope in Darby's bold, haphazard handwriting. She tucked the letter in her pocket, not yet strong enough for the pain its contents would surely bring.

Later that night, when the moon was full in the sky and the air was filled with the soft symphony of crickets and katydids, Willy carried the letter to the riverbank and began to read.

> *Willy,*
>
> *The day I saw you walking with your umbrella, I loved you.*
>
> *I loved the soft curve of your cheek, and the sunlight in your hair, and the soft music of your voice. I was hypnotized by the beauty and the sheer wonder of you. Days*

turned into weeks, and my love for you grew until my heart could no longer contain it. Tonight, as I sit, missing you, longing for you, I know that no man has ever loved a woman more.

Do not cry for me, Willy, for I am an old man. I have seen eight decades come and go. Do not grieve, for I have been privileged to live my life as a young man. And though I wanted to believe that love would be enough to sustain us, I have known from the start that it would not and could not be so. Trapped here, within the boundaries of this land, you would have been like a beautiful butterfly encased in glass, unable to fly. In the end you would have come to resent the life we dreamed of. Like me, you would grow to see the blessing as a curse. I want you to soar, Willy. I want you to live and love and be beautiful, unafraid. The years will bring you joy, as well as pain. Embrace it all. Embrace it for as many years as you are granted on this earth.

Dearest Willy, know that you have brought me joy and comfort. Your love has been all that any man could want, and far more than this man deserves. Keep my memory alive in your heart, and know that I will love you...

Until the end of time.
Darby

~ * ~

Anger welled up inside her as she read and reread the words. Tearing the medallion from its chain, she clasped it in her fist and shook it at the sky.

"You had no right!" she screamed. Her words echoed across the river, then returned to her. "You had no right to make that decision for me... for us!"

She drew back her fist, intending to hurl the medallion into the river. From somewhere far away she heard a dog bark, and her hand dropped back to her side. Tears streamed from her eyes as she searched the shadows around her.

"Lucky?" she called softly. "Is it you?"

She heard him walking in the woods, felt his presence drawing near. She saw no evidence of him, but she knew that Darby stood before her.

"You had no right," she whispered.

It started as a warm glow, then became an electric heat, wrapping her from head to toe. It was love in its purest form, and she clung to it.

"Please, Darby," she sobbed, "don't leave me all alone."

A gentle breeze lifted her hair like a caress, whispering in her ear.

"Shhhh."

All that night she lay on the riverbank, wrapped in the blanket of his love. When the morning sun broke through the clouds, she awoke, and he was gone.

Twenty Four

The letter arrived five days after Willy's return home from the hospital: a brusque greeting on crisp, white paper that informed her she had seven days to vacate the property. She stared at the words at the top of the page, spelled out in bold black: By order of the Department of Parks and Recreations.

She'd known her days in Baker's Gully were numbered, but even so, the decree hit her with the force of a punch in the stomach. She carried it to the phone and dialed Zoe's number, rereading the letter as her call rang through.

Zoe listened quietly as she spoke, and there was a long pause in which Willy could almost see the attorney collecting and organizing her thoughts.

"What do you think?" Willy prompted.

"I guess I'm trying to understand your reasons for wanting to stay there," she said.

Now it was Willy's turn to be silent. How could she explain? How could a practical, analytical mind like Zoe's possibly understand?

She hadn't felt Darby's physical presence since the night she read his letter, but even so, she felt close to him here. Here, on this land that had been so much a part of him, the Eden where they'd laughed and loved together. It was as though his very thumbprint were imprinted on the landscape.

"I'm just not ready to leave yet, Zoe."

Zoe sighed. "What was the original term of your lease?"

"Six months. June to November."

"Let me make a few phone calls. At the very least, the realtors might have to refund the balance of your money."

"Thanks, Zoe."

Zoe called her back later that afternoon.

"Okay, here's the deal. The Parks Department is going to honor the lease for two more months. You have until October first. Hanrahan will refund the extra two months rent you paid. Best I can do."

Relief flooded through her. She still had time. "Thanks, Zoe."

"Just doing my job, kid." Zoe paused. "Are you sure you're all right up there, Willy?"

Willy knew what she was asking. Sid had taken to calling three times a day, convinced that Willy was living in a fantasy world, that she was sitting on her porch, talking to the moon and slowly driving herself mad.

"I'm fine."

"Okay," Zoe said, in a tone that betrayed doubt. "Call us if you need anything."

August passed in a leisurely succession of golden days and cool, quiet nights. Willy passed her days in varying stages of pain and numbness, stealing off to the woods beyond the river, where she could quietly nurse her broken spirit and photograph nature in all its silent splendor. When her divorce decree arrived in the mail, on the fifteenth day of the month, she glanced at it with a detached sense of relief. She could get on with her life now, as the saying went. But for Willy, life no longer held and meaning.

~ * ~

Autumn arrived early in Baker's Gully.

Overnight, the air turned crisp, and the treetops were tinted with hints of orange, yellow, and deep scarlet. Other changes were taking place, as well. The sound of heavy equipment rumbled across the valley as dozers and backhoes began to clear the land on the other side of the river. The raped landscape cried out for vengeance, and Mother Nature took heed. It rained for six days straight. After that, Willy took to walking in the gully, carefully avoiding the empty hole where Darby's cabin used to be.

In the last week of September, she went walking in the field beyond her house, collecting armloads of cattails and teasel to be dried and set in vases on the porch. Walking back to the cottage in the early afternoon, she was startled to see an unfamiliar car parked in her driveway and quickened her pace.

The Parks Department, no doubt, coming to remind me I have less than a week to vacate, she thought with a flash of irritation. She marched around to the back of the house, and froze, her heart nearly stopping when she saw the man standing on her back porch.

His hair was more copper than brown, but the gray eyes behind the wire rims of his glasses were kind and beautiful and heartbreakingly familiar. Broad shoulders tapered down to a lean waist, and muscular arms hung loosely at his sides. Her first thought was to fling herself into them, but she stopped herself.

Hearing her approach, the man turned, his full lips turning up in an endearing, lopsided smile. "Are you Willow?" he asked, in a voice that had the rich texture of fine brandy. "Willow Mackenzie?"

Unable to speak, she nodded, and his smile grew wider.

"I'm happy to meet you, Willow. My name is Patrick." He extended a hand and she reached for it. It was free of calluses, but warm and powerful, just the same.

"What can I do for you, Patrick?"

"If it wouldn't be too much of an inconvenience..." he faltered. "I mean, I can see that you're busy, but if you have a moment, I was hoping to talk with you for a little while."

"About?"

"About my great-uncle, Darby Sullivan."

Twenty Five

He regarded her for a long moment, his eyes gently probing her face. "I'm sorry, have I upset you?"

Foolish tears sprang to her eyes at the mention of her lover's name, and she quickly blinked them away. "What is it you'd like to discuss, Mr.... Patrick?"

"Sullivan. Patrick Sullivan. It's kind of a long story." He indicated the table. "Can we sit?"

She saw how uncomfortable she'd made him and realized then how rude she must seem, standing there like a statue, staring at him. "Yes, please do. I have a pot of mulled cider simmering on the stove. Would you like a glass?"

He rewarded her with another lopsided smile. "Sounds good."

In the kitchen, she retrieved two mugs from the cupboard and set them on a tray with a pair of plates and the apple spice cake she'd made the day before. She grabbed a pair of forks from the drawer, set them on the plates, and carried the tray to the porch.

Patrick stood when she appeared. "You didn't have to go to so much trouble, Willow. Let me get that for you."

"You can call me Willy. And it's no trouble." She set the tray down on the table and slid into the seat across from him. "Help yourself."

He poured two glasses of cider and handed her one before taking a swallow. "Mmmm. Very nice. What's in it?"

"Cloves, cinnamon, orange peel. I can never quite remember the formula, so it's kind of hit or miss every time."

"Well, it's definitely a hit, this time," he said, tipping his mug toward hers in a toast. Willy set her mug down and folded her hands on the table, waiting to hear the reason for his visit.

As if reading her thoughts, he cleared his throat. "I'm a history teacher at Thomas Jefferson High School in Bridgeton. It's just the other side of Colbert."

"I know where Bridgeton is," Willy said.

"You're familiar with the city, then?"

"I grew up on the west side. Dobbler Park."

He paused to digest the information before continuing. "Last year I assigned my students the task of tracing their family trees. I thought I ought to practice what I preach, so I started digging around in my own lineage. Once I got started, I got so wrapped up in it I couldn't seem to stop."

~ * ~

He told her about his great-grandparents, Quinn and Maggie Sullivan, and how they'd emigrated to the United States from Ireland in the hope of a better life. They fled to Chicago when the Depression hit, desperate to find work in the factories. They'd taken their two-year-old daughter, Ellie, and their infant son, Brody, but had been forced to leave their other two children behind.

Willy watched his eyes as he spoke, kind, wise eyes. His speech was that of an educated man, the tones deeper than Darby's, but if she closed her eyes, it was almost as though...

"Anyway," he said, startling her from her thoughts. "Sophia died in the hospital of pneumonia shortly after they left, and Darby was placed in a home in West Dover. A farm called Brookhaven. I drove out there this morning to investigate, and noticed your name in the register at the historical society. Listed beside it was the last known address for Darby Sullivan. I asked the gentleman who runs the place about you, and he told me you'd been there to research your grandfather's childhood. I got excited, thinking I might have a long-lost cousin, and here I am."

"I'm sorry to have to disappoint you, Patrick, but Darby was not my grandfather. We aren't related at all."

"Now that I've met you, I can't say I'm disappointed." A blush crept up his face, and he abruptly continued.

"Quinn Sullivan died of lung disease a few years later, and Maggie's health began to suffer from the deplorable work conditions in the factory. Story is, she always meant to come back for her children. Penniless and in poor health, it broke her heart that she couldn't. She went to her grave at age forty wondering what happened to them.

"He would have liked to have known that," Willy said softly. "That she never forgot him." She started to choke up and fought for control. "I'm sorry, Patrick. If you've come here looking for Darby, you're too late. He passed away last month."

"You knew him?"

"Yes."

"What sort of fellow was he?"

Willy took a breath. "Strong. Kind. Generous." She absently fingered the medallion. "He was a wonderful man."

Patrick's gaze lingered on her face. "He must have been."

A heaviness settled over them and he steered the conversation back to her.

"So... you grew up on the west side?"

She gave him a brief sketch of her childhood,

glossing over the ugliness. She told him about her years at the university, and her job at the magazine.

"Sounds fascinating," he said. "Why did you leave?"

She shrugged. "I had some unexpected health problems. This seemed like a good place to recuperate."

"Nothing serious, I hope?"

She held his gaze for a moment, then looked away. "Nothing I can't survive."

He told her about his boyhood in Chicago, and how he'd come to New York to go to college.

"And you never left?" she asked, genuinely curious.

"I fell in love with the area, and a young lady. I got a job, got married. You know how the story goes." He fiddled with his glass. "The marriage wasn't one of my better decisions. It lasted less than a year, but I stayed in love with the city."

He glanced at his watch. "I should go. I've taken up enough of your time.'

She walked him to his car. He took a moment to comment on the landscape, and the weather, as if reluctant to leave. Finally, he shifted uncomfortably, and blurted, "I'm really bad at this."

"Bad at what?"

"I'd like to see you again, Willy. I enjoyed your company very much." Once again, a blush crept across his face. Suddenly, he was like a shy little boy, and she found him hard to refuse.

"I'm going to be moving back to the city soon. Maybe we can arrange something."

His face brightened. "Call me when you get settled, then. I'd like to take you out to dinner." He opened his wallet, pulled out a business card and handed it to her. She glanced at the front: *Personal Tutoring, Patrick Sullivan, MS Ed. Reasonable Rates.*

"I'll do that," she said, tucking the card in her

pocket.

She stood in the driveway, watching long after his car had disappeared from sight.

Twenty Six

At eight o'clock on the last Saturday in September, Sid's Neon pulled into Willy's driveway. After a breakfast of Belgian waffles and home fries, she and Willy began the task of packing up the cottage.

"You're going to love this house, Willy." Sid tore a sheet of newspaper from the stack in front of her, wrapped a dinner plate, and set it in a box marked *kitchen.* "It's just far enough from the city that it's peaceful, and just close enough that it's convenient."

She grabbed another plate, wrapped it, and placed it in the box. "It's got three bathrooms and four fireplaces, did I tell you? And your room has a little balcony that looks out over the garden."

"It sounds great, Sid." Willy removed a grapevine wreath from the wall, wrapped it, and set it in a box. "I feel terrible imposing on you and Zoe, though. Good Lord, talk about a third wheel."

"Don't be ridiculous. We're going to charge you an outrageous amount of rent. And anyway, once you start back at the magazine, Milo will have you off globetrotting again and we'll never see you."

Having idled away the last few weeks of summer, Willy brightened at the prospect of returning to work. She'd worked up the nerve to call Milo a few days before to feel him out about the possibility of returning to the magazine part-time. She was relieved and immensely pleased at how quickly he'd agreed to take her back.

"It'll be good to be busy," she said, more to herself than Sid. She gazed out the window, already feeling a pang of loneliness for the river, the gently sloping hillside.

Sid set down her stack of plates and came to Willy's side. "You okay?"

"It's going to seem strange, after all that's happened. I'll be going back to my old life, but everything's different now." She brushed away a stray tear. "I miss him."

"Oh, sweetie, I know." Sid wrapped her arms around her and held her for a long moment.

Willy pushed her gloomy thoughts aside and forced a smile.

"We'd better get back at it. Chance will be here first thing in the morning."

~ * ~

They worked quickly, and by late afternoon all of Willy's possessions were boxed, labeled, and neatly stacked in the kitchen.

Looking around the empty rooms, Willy sighed. "We did it."

"Yep."

"We deserve a break. Feel like coffee?"

"I have a better idea," Sid said, grinning wickedly. "I passed a little place outside of town that had a big sign advertising hot apple sundaes. What do you say?"

"Ahhh, I say let me get my purse."

As they were climbing into the Explorer, a van pulled into the driveway behind them.

"Expecting company?" Sid asked, eyebrows raised.

"No." Puzzled, Willy got out and walked to the van.

The driver put down his window. "You Willow

Mackenzie?"

"Yes."

"You're a tough lady to find. I've got a delivery for you."

Curious, Willy peered over his shoulder while he opened the back of the van. Within moments he retrieved an enormous bouquet of fall flowers: coppery mums and golden sunflowers, their vibrant colors offset with pale, apricot-colored asters and variegated autumn leaves.

Willy's breath caught. "Oh, how lovely. Are you sure that's for me?"

"It is if you're Willow Mackenzie," he said. Handing her a clipboard, he pointed at the dotted line on the delivery slip. "Sign here."

She signed the paper, and he tore off the top copy and handed it to her, then got into his van and drove away without another word. Willy pressed her face into the bouquet, inhaling its sweet, earthy scent.

"Holy Moses, look at the size of that bouquet," Sid exclaimed. "Someone gave up some serious coinage for that."

There was a card attached, and Willy opened it, Sid peering over her shoulder as she read:

> *Willy,*
>> *Looking forward to seeing you soon.*
>> *Patrick*

Sid grinned. "So who's Patrick?"

"Just a guy."

"Just a guy with excellent taste in flowers. And women."

Willy smiled. "I'd better run these in the house."

"Is he anyone?" Sid called after her.

"I don't know." She called over her shoulder.

"Maybe."

~ * ~

Willy awoke the next morning at six a.m. to overcast skies and a light, misting rain. She dressed quickly in a pair of jeans and sweatshirt, then slipped quietly out of the house.

Walking along the riverbank, memories flooded over her, bringing joy and sadness. Like cherished children, she gathered them to her, treasuring them, writing them across her heart. At last she allowed her gaze to linger on the vacant plot of land where Darby's cabin had been. She allowed herself to relive the memory of his laughter, his eyes, and the feel of his hand in hers. She whispered the truth, over and over, until her heart heard, and finally accepted it.

He's gone...

Back home, Chance had arrived with a box of doughnuts and three steaming cups of coffee. After a quick breakfast, they moved the boxes and the furniture outside and loaded them into the back of the delivery van.

"All right, ladies," Chance said, when the last piece had been loaded. "Guess I'll see you on the flip side." He kissed Willy's cheek. "I'm really glad you're coming back, babe."

As the van disappeared down the road, Sid turned to her.

"Are we ready?"

"I'll catch up with you, Sid," Willy said. "There's something I have to do."

"Okay, but don't be too long. I'm dying for you to see the house."

She drove off with a blast of her horn, leaving Willy alone in the driveway. Bracing herself, she went back inside. After a last walk through the cottage, she grabbed the bouquet of flowers from off the counter. Pulling the door closed behind her, she got in her Explorer and drove away, not allowing herself to look back.

~ * ~

Just beyond the village of Murphy's Crossing, she made a left-hand turn onto a graveled road. Rain fell steadily and she slowed to a crawl, peering through the wipers at each crossroads she came to. Finally she found the road she was looking for.

She turned onto the tree-lined street and pulled into the entrance of Clearview Cemetery. Leaving the Explorer in the grassy lot, she wandered among the headstones, glancing at the names, until she came to an unmarked grave beneath the shade of a crimson maple tree. A military cross bearing his dates of service perched beside a small, plain grave marker.

Willy sank to her knees and placed her fingers in the freshly turned dirt. The only words spoken were those communicated from her heart. She knelt beside his grave in a solemn, silent memorial as the rain continued to fall.

Finally, she removed the medallion from around her neck. It was cool and silent in her palm, its surface mottled, and Willy knew that it no longer held any power; that her healing was not in this bit of tarnished metal, but in the love with which it had been given. Parting the earth with her hands, she lovingly placed the medallion inside. When the last of her tears had been spent, she placed the bouquet on Darby's grave and stood to leave.

Walking back to her truck, she heard the low, far-off sound of a dog's barking. She turned back, her eyes scanning the landscape. A shadow fell across her, and her gaze was drawn upward, in the direction of a shrill, piercing cry.

She watched, breathless, as an eagle circled in the sky above her with a magnificent flourish of wings and feathers. The eagle, with its power and mystery and majesty. The eagle. The only animal brave enough to stare into the face of the sun.

With a haunting cry, it began its upward ascent. It

was then that Willy recalled the old Welsh legend her grandmother used to tell, that of departing souls flying to heaven in the form of eagles. With a mounting sense of elation, she watched as it climbed into the heavens and disappeared.

"It's you," she whispered. "Isn't it?"

As if in answer, the skies opened up and drenched her with rain, and she opened her arms and embraced it. Crystal beads clung to her hair and ran into her mouth and over her body, washing away her guilt and pain and doubt. Joy welled up inside of her, and she knew that, like the eagle, she could soar. Love and hope existed in the world, and on the wings of it, she could face the future unafraid.

She'd spent all of her life waiting for the rain, and now, at last, the storm had passed, and everything was brighter in its wake.

About Jean

Restless spirits. Abandoned buildings. Love that lasts forever. These are a few of M. Jean Pike's favorite things. A professional writer since 1996, Ms. Pike combines a passion for romance with a keen interest in the supernatural to bring readers unforgettable tales of life, love, and the inner workings of the human heart. She writes from her home on a quiet country road in beautiful upstate New York.

Visit our website for our growing catalogue of quality books.
www.champagnebooks.com

Printed in the United States
152814LV00001B/2/A

9 781897 445211